# ANGEL

## The Road Rangers MC

# M.D. LABELLE

This is for all of you smut sluts who love hand necklaces, gun play, obsessed masked men, rough sex and smoking hot bikers covered in tattoos.  You know who you are.

M.D. LaBelle

## Some of M.D. LaBelle's Other Books and Book Series

The Defiant Collection

Forbidden Kiss

Just Love Me The Bad Behavior Series

Cursed Blood

The Luna's Mate: The Alpha King

Sophia

Valentine

Meant To Be: The Violinist's Tale

The Circus

The Casper's Firsts Series

And Many More

## Chapter 1: The Beginning

On one warm summer's night loud gun shots echo throughout the heat of the night. High pitched screams are heard as several women scatter and hide behind the motorcycles as just another drug deal goes bad. When all is said and done, one man lies dead as his body slowly grows cold and his blood soaks into the hard ground.

---

4 Years later and several cities away.

"Hello. Is this Brandon?" A voice that sounds strangely familiar to me asks hesitantly.

As I stand there staring at the unlisted number, I suddenly get this nagging feeling that this woman is from my sordid past, so I reply cautiously, "Yes. May I ask who this is?"

Immediately, my muscles tense when she says, "Amy. Do you remember me?"

Of course, I do. How could I forget? Four years ago, I had left the Road Rangers Motor Club because I had seen far too many people die that I cared about. I had refused to lose anyone else, and I decided that the only way to do that was to leave and pursue something better, something legal for a change.

After leaving my brother Drift in charge, I drove away and had high hopes that I would never hear from any of them again. However, apparently, something had happened, or they would not have gone against my wishes.

"Amy. I remember you. You are Drift's woman, aren't you? Or at least you were when I left. You and Drift were the only ones who knew what my real name was."

I hesitate and then add, "By the way, how is that old man? I sure wouldn't have thought that he would have lasted this long. Not the way he was going."

There is silence for a moment and then I hear her sigh before she replies softly, "That is sort of the problem. Drift is dead."

Another pause and then she states sadly, "We need you. Everyone is fighting and about to start a huge gang war. No one is strong enough to take over without everyone else going after him. They won't vote for a single person because everyone wants to be the leader. Please. Please come back. Even if it is only for a short time, it is better than nothing because I am afraid that everything, we have worked so hard to accomplish will be gone if someone doesn't step up right now."

While feeling the shock of what she just said, I shut my eyes at first to fight away the pain. But then I swallow hard and stare blankly down at the phone. Honestly, I should have known that this would eventually happen, but to hear it, hit me harder than I thought it would. As for the last part of her statement, I need to think about it. So, I cock my head and furrow my brow as I contemplate this and then quickly bury it in the back of my mind before I say bitterly, "No. I am sorry for your troubles, but I won't. Now that Drift is gone, there is nothing tying me to the past. In a way, I am glad."

When I abruptly end the call, I don't say goodbye because there is simply no point. I can't afford to care anymore. I did that once and look where that got me. Instead, I slip the phone onto the nightstand and pull back the covers. It will be a long night now, but I must get some sleep before tomorrow. That life is in the past and I just wished that it had stayed that way. However, the moment my head hits the pillow, I can already tell that it will eat away at me until I do something.

I sigh while lying there, staring at the ceiling, and wishing that things had not just suddenly changed. How dare he die and leave me to pick up the pieces. He knew that was the farthest thing from what I wanted.

"Urgh." I cry out into the darkness of the room as I bolt up in bed and stare at the looming shadows that waltz across the walls.

A moment later I walk to the bathroom and find myself staring at my haggard reflection in the medicine cabinet mirror. The steam from the hot water begins to fog up the image as I wipe it away and shake my head. Before me is what most women would describe as a relatively handsome man in his 30's staring back at me with tired light blue eyes and badly in need of a shave. I murmur under my breath, "It figures. Just when I thought I had a handle on life, something has to throw a monkey wrench into the gears."

I breathe in deeply and then yell at the top of my lungs, "Fuck."

I guess I should call her back and see when the funeral is. At least then I can survey the situation and figure out what if anything I could possibly do to fix it."

After I wash my face off and dry it with the towel hanging next to the sink, I shut the hot water off and realize what time it is as I look up at the clock on the wall. It's 3:50 a.m. Good God it's early. This will have to wait until the morning.

I don't know how, but at some point, I manage to fall asleep as I stare at the ceiling while lying naked under the crisp white cotton sheets. When I hear the neighbor's door slam shut, my eyes pop open and I realize that it is later than I had hoped for.

"Shit!" I exclaim while sitting up in bed and stretching my muscular arms above my head.

No more than a moment later, I slip out from under the covers and look around to find the clothes I had carelessly thrown on the floor the night before. Unfortunately, as I do this, I notice that I have an enormous hard on and it begins to ache incredibly painfully as I walk back and forth. Right now, is hardly the time for this, but it is what it is, so I sit down on the edge of the bed and close my eyes.

When my fingers grasp the hard shaft like a stick shift, they begin to slide up and down the length stiffly as my other hand tightens around my throbbing balls. A deep moan erupts from my throat when my thumb grazes the tip and I imagine Janine's expert lips on my head as she swallows him down whole. I fucking love when she deep throats him and chokes. It gets me even hotter. I think to myself as I lick my lips slowly and throw my head back while I feel my thick cock jerk in my hands.

Usually, while her lips are on my head, I wrap my fingers in her silky blonde hair and force her down quickly on him. It makes me shutter every time and my dick jerks as her tongue licks it. That shit always feels so damn good.

Just thinking about it makes my hand tighten around him, then I feel him swell as I pick up the pace. My palm slides up and down again and again while I squeeze my balls tighter until I can swear, they will pop but they don't. Instead, it builds deep within me and my blood pressure boils.

Suddenly, I stop and tighten my grip on him as I feel the pressure start to become unbearable. Then my breathing speeds up and all I can think about is her perfect tits as I slide my dick right between them and squirt all over her unusually beautiful face.

"Fuck. You are such a dirty girl." I yell as I begin to stroke him again dry and methodically.

"I am going to fuck you right in that tight little ass of yours next." I murmur as my balls get harder and harder. Then and only then, do I feel a surge of adrenalin right before my hot cum shoots clear across the bedroom and hits the wall. "Ughhh" I cry out as I shut my eyelids and throw my head back in ecstasy.

A shiver runs up my spine as I continue to fist him until he becomes soft. Afterwards, I quickly take a shower and find myself staring in the mirror at the length of my tattooed body in admiration. It took years to get every one of them, but it was worth it because I am now a living tribute to all of those I have lost.

Once I get dressed, I pick up my phone and quickly call my boss to tell her of my brothers' death. Mrs. Fields gives me the week off to attend the funeral and to mourn. But what she doesn't know is that if things turn out the way I suspect they will, I won't be coming back at all. I guess Mrs. Fields will just have to find another full-time chauffeur to fulfill her needs.

After I locate Amy's number in the call log, I call her back and find out that Drift's funeral is today at 4 p.m. That gives me little time to pack and to get there, but I will just make it if I hurry. The last thing I do before I leave with my duffel bag of clothes and the few items I care about, is to say goodbye to my one and only friendly neighbor Sandy. Just in case I never see her again, I give her a huge hug and then thank her for being there for me.

As I get on my bike, I look back one last time to the place I have called home for the last 4 years. Then I ride like the wind and hope that time is on my side for once.

## Chapter 2: Justine Masterson

"Oh, mom. Todd cheated on me." I cry out as I kneel on one knee in front of her grave.

"I suppose I should have known that he was all wrong for me, but he was the only one who knew the real me." I say sadly as I wipe a few tears out of the corners of my eyes.

Every year, on the same day I come here to visit my mom's grave and I always have to lie to my grandparents, so they will not want to come with me. They just don't understand that I need time alone with her, to get things off my chest that I normally would have been able to tell her if she were still alive. Four years ago, she was murdered during a bad drug deal. Honestly, I don't care what it was because I still lost her no matter what the circumstances.

All I know is that my family was at war with another rivel biker gang. I never saw it because I have lived with my grandparents since I was little. But when my mom wasn't spending the winters with us, she was with them. Because of that, I have always hated my dad and his gang.

As I grew older, I could see how hard it was on my grandparents every time she left us. Now as for my dad, I have only met him once and I wished I never had, because I could tell that I didn't like him from the moment he set eyes upon me. That was the summer that he dragged her out the door and I never saw her again.

At the age of 29, I suppose I could be doing more with my life, but what really is the point? Besides, my grandparents pretty much begged me to stay with them so they could keep an eye on me. Plus, there is always the fact that I hear their whispers of worry when they say I am becoming my mother and father.

After wiping another stray tear off my cheek, I look down at the beautiful red and blue tattoo on my forearm. I remember later that summer when I got it in remembrance of her, it was hot, and the sun was so bright that it was hard to stay sad for too long.

"I don't know if I will be here next year or not because I have had a job offer in Tennessee that I may take. If I do, it will be a few years before I can get back out here again and visit you. I hope you won't mind too much but I will always keep you in my thoughts." I murmur under my breath as I watch one last motorcycle pull up and a tall, masked man climb off in a designer suit.

As I watch him take his mask off and then join the others, I notice that he is handsome but looks so out of place among all the other bikers in their black leather outfits and jeans. "How odd." I whisper as I rub my hand over the rough edge of the gravestone.

I cock my head as I stare in their direction for a moment too long and I see him glance over at me. Our eyes lock and I feel this instant electricity as if I stuck my finger in an electric socket. It feels powerful but no more than two seconds later when he looks away, it is gone.

A few minutes before the connection, I had watched him hold a baby and for some reason that seemed so strange to me. Is that baby his? And that his woman? More importantly, why do I even care?

I shake my head and glance down at my phone as I remember why I am here. "Mom, I love you so much. I promise I will never forget you." I say softly as I stand up and take a step back.

"I need to get going because grandma and grandpa have made a special dinner on your behalf. I guess it is their way of honoring your memory. Hopefully, next year I will be back. If not, I will be here when I can. You know I will." I whisper and then my voice trails off before I head back to my car.

Not only is it a cooler than normal day for California, but it seems as if darkness has set around me. So, hopefully if I get this job, it won't follow me to Tennessee, and I can start a new life. So many possibilities.

Before I shut the door and drive off, I glance over one last time to where the man is standing. I stop and stare because he is looking right at me and watching my every move. When his eyes raise to mine, that electricity returns. Does he feel it too? Surely, he does because a second later he looks away and begins to talk with the woman next to him.

So strange, but before I can even entertain anything, he heads in the opposite direction towards another group of bikers. Of course, I had let myself get my hopes up, so I swallow hard and shut the door as quickly as I can before driving off. After all, there is a difference between dreaming and what is real. In all reality, that man probably is married to her, and that baby is his.

All the way home, I couldn't stop thinking about the look he gave me. And as soon as I open the front door, the smells from the kitchen surround me. I lick my lips and instantly my stomach starts growling. I love my grandmother's cooking more than most things on this earth. "Now that is the best thing." I murmur under my breath because I love to come back to the smell of a homemade blueberry pie in the oven.

"Are you there?" Grandma Ellen asks softly before she peers around the corner of the kitchen.

"Yes, grandma. Something smells deeeelicious."

"Well, I think dinner is ready. Why don't you call Grandpa to the table? I think he is out back cutting wood." Grandma says sweetly as she cuts the homemade buttermilk bread.

I smile at her and then give her a hug before I walk to the back door and open it. I yell out, "Grandpa. Dinner is ready."

A moment later, I watch as he walks around the corner of the barn, and I see a smile spread across his face from ear to ear. "You don't have to call me twice." He replies as he quickens his pace and meets me at the door.

Once he hugs me and pats my back, we take our seats at the table and grandma brings in the glazed ham.

## Chapter 3: Old Habits Die Hard

When I see the old wooden city limits sign for Crescent Bay, I swallow hard because it's been too long. I swear that I will always remember that sign until the day I die. Crescent Bay is a small coastal town just outside of San Francisco.

It is beautiful but also dangerous because it is home to the Road Rangers MC, my real family. At the time of my departure, we were still running guns and drugs into the city. However, things may have changed since I left. Or at least I hope they have.

The moment I see the old-fashioned streetlights, I know I am home, and that things really don't change in these tiny towns. Even though most of those who used to live here had moved on when we took over.

"The same old same old." I murmur under my breath as I rev the engine and speed down the road towards the cemetery.

It will be a closed casket so there will be no funeral in a church. Just the sermon at St. Joseph's. It is the only cemetery in the vicinity so I know exactly where everyone will be. As I speed around the last corner before it, a fleeting memory flashes through my mind of when I was foolish and young. Of when I thought I ruled the world.

I remember what the old leader had said one night before he died as we sat around a campfire and drank whiskey from the bottle. He told me that I could fuck his women, but I could never touch his bike because that is the only thing that matters. That was funny to me at the time. However, when I lost my oldest brother to the harsh reality of our lifestyle 4 years earlier, I had to grow up quicker than I had hoped and realized what he had really meant by that.

By that time, mom and dad were already gone and I wasn't willing to watch as my other brother Drift lost his life as well. However, for a short time longer, I was their leader, but I knew that I couldn't stay forever. Especially, when my careless behavior led to my own brother's death.

---

As I ride into the driveway, I see all the other bikes lined up in two rows almost a half mile long. So, I quickly take my place behind them, then I climb off and hang my skull mask on the handle before I hike up to everyone else. Immediately, they size me up with wide eyes.

I guess they did not think I would come or that anyone had gotten ahold of me because I could register the shock on all their faces when I show up in my tailored black dress suit that technically belongs to my boss. It makes me look so out of place among all the bikers in their black leather.

"So, the prodigal son returns alright. That's just fucking wonderful." Austin says sarcastically as he slaps me on the back a little too hard to be meant as welcoming.

I swivel around on my heels and reply snidely, "Oh, you are using big words now? Clearly, you must have learned a thing or two while I was gone."

He looks at me for a few minutes as we stand there silently sizing each other up. Then suddenly a smile forms on his lips and he smacks me on the back again, but this time I can tell that he is purely fucking around.

"Man, I have missed you. So, did you just come back for this or for good? Because we sure could use a leader that will put everyone back in their places. In case you missed it, there has been a war going on between us all and it is getting tiresome." He says softly now as he gives me a big hug.

After he steps back and looks over to where the casket is, I run my hand through my hair and reply quietly, "Yeah, I heard. I don't know yet how long I will be here. After all, I wasn't planning on staying because I do have a new life now and even a real job."

As I stare at him for a few seconds, I realize that he really hasn't changed too much except for the fact that he has let his black hair grow out and he now has a beard to match.

"Man, I am just glad you are here. I happen to know of a little lady who will be happy too. Amy has always thought of you as a little bro and Drift's death has hit her the hardest. Did you know that they got married last year? And she has a baby. Why, that means you are an uncle." Austin says as he smiles brightly and points over to where

Amy is sitting in the row of chairs directly in front of the casket.

It looks like the ceremony is about to start before they place him in the ground, so I quickly state, "Speaking of that, I want to thank her for getting ahold of me before this whole thing starts."

He looks between me and Amy and then says sadly, "Oh yeah. I should let you get to that then."

After smacking me on the shoulder, he walks with me up to where she is seated. There is an empty seat next to her and I take it before anyone else does. When she turns around to face me, she practically throws the baby in my arms as she says, "Oh Angel, I don't know what I am going to do. Drift was supposed to take care of us. Now, I am a widow and a new mother all at the same time. I don't know what to do. Please, please tell me that you are going to stay and get everything settled once and for all."

I lower my eyes as I speak because I really don't know if I should. But then I reply softly, "Amy, I am sorry about this, but I am just not too sure that it would be the right thing for me to do. I have been away for so long. I can't even pretend to know what is going on anymore. I am a changed man, and I don't know if I even have it in me anymore."

She looks at me with tear-stained eyes and pleads with me, "Please. You must. I know that Drift would want you to."

No matter how low that was for her to play the Drift card, I keep my cool and wipe the tears from her cheek with my thumb before I kiss her forehead and state, "I will try. That is all I can guarantee. After all, if I hadn't left, my brother would still be alive, and I'd be the one in this casket right now. I owe him that at least."

Realizing the commitment I just made, I slink down in my seat to scan the area before I return my gaze to the little one to the side of me.

"Meet Jonathan. Come on, hold him. After all, he is your nephew." She says as she hands him to me carefully.

I wrap my arms around him and suddenly feel so huge compared to this tiny human that is staring at me with the bluest eyes I have ever seen. It's amazing that such a small thing could make me feel a sudden urge to protect it with all my being. So, as I sit next to her and we both stare at Drift's casket, the preacher walks up and starts to say a few words.

## Chapter 4: Drift's Last Ride

"He was a strong leader and a good man if there ever was one." The minister says as he looks down at me for a second.

After he ruffles his papers around, he looks up and stares at the crowd before he adds, "I won't spout on about bible verses and a long sermon because Drift never put too much stock into the Lord, and I doubt that any of you have either. As a matter of fact, I pretty much guarantee that if he had his way, he is looking up at you, because he often told me that he would rather rock on with the sinners than go to heaven and be bored with all the saints."

Jim Hawthorn or shall we say the good minister, grew up with us and we all played together as kids. But we split ways when we took over the family business. He, of course, decided that we were not the kind of people he necessarily wanted to be associated with when he became a minister. So, frankly, I am quite surprised that he is the one speaking here today for Drift.

"Now is there anyone here that wants to say a few words before we wrap up and bury him." he says quickly while glancing around the crowd.

It is at that point that I feel everyone's eyes on me as if no one else wants to be the one. Fine, I guess I should consider, it is my brother and all. Although, I don't have a clue what to say because I have been out of the loop for so long.

As I try to come up with anything, I stand up and straighten out my suit before I walk up to the tiny podium by the grave. I look out over the crowd and suddenly feel choked up. These are the people I used to call my family and I had deserted them. I had no more right to speak than the minister. But as I look over each of them, I realize one thing. We have all lost too much and things need to change.

"Drift was a good man in his own way. He became the best man he could in his circumstances. When I left, I had decided never to come back. I had my own reasons as you all well know, but I didn't think that he would be leaving us so soon or I may have changed my mind. I remember when we were kids and he always looked out for me. Well, now it is time again for me to look out for all of you because you are all family. He tried to make things better for everyone, and for a little while he may have. Thank you, brother, for being you. That was all I could have asked for." I say softly as I stare down at the casket and the hole in the ground.

Because I have no more to say, I take my seat again and watch as they begin to slowly lower the casket down. It is a somber event, but these things always are. I just can't let my feelings take over right now because I have unfinished business to take care of.

After turning to gaze at Amy I realize that the only thing left to do is regain control of the organization. It should be relatively easy considering I had already been the head once. But will everyone follow me willingly or will I be forced to prove that I am still a capable leader? That is the question.

"Amy, can I stay with you tonight? This was all so sudden, and I don't really have any place else." I ask softly as I watch a few of the riders begin to disperse.

She nods, and then we stand to leave. However, when I look over and see a woman staring at me by a gravestone, I feel this uneasiness and I don't know why. Oddly enough, she is a drop dead gorgeous raven-haired beauty who is so pale that she looks as if she had spent all her life inside. "What wouldn't I do to run my hands over that porcelain skin?" I murmur under my breath as my cock jerks to life in my pants.

"Do you know her?" I ask hesitantly as I point her out to Amy.

Immediately, she stops in her tracks and doesn't say a word, just stares on.
"What is it?" I continue to ask because now I am sure there is something wrong.

She turns away so I can't see her eyes before she murmurs sadly, "That is the daughter of the rival gang leader. She will only bring you trouble. Leave it be."

With that said, we turn around and walk towards the others. The last thing I need right now is more complications.

"So, who do I have to kill around here to get everyone to stop this shit?" I ask sarcastically as I smack Tiny on the back.

He looks down at me with a shit eating grin before he answers snidely, "Well. If you are referring to the fighting, that won't happen until you take over again."

"Really? I swear I can't leave you all alone for more than a couple of years or you would tear each other apart."

"I know, but that was the last straw. They intervened in our drug deal, and they had to pay." Tiny replies quickly as he puts on his helmet.

"Well, there must be another way. We need to go legal, so we don't get killed over the littlest thing. After all, I am an uncle now and I need to look out for everyone's best interest. That means no drug running anymore and we get a legitimate business. Guns are always a hot commodity. So why not legal gun dealers? We can do this." I say quietly so no one else accidentally overhears us.

## Chapter 5: Amy's Place

We talk with everyone for a while but then I hear Jonathan start to cry and look over at Amy. She seems tired so I state quickly, "Well, I think it is time to head out. I will be staying at Amy's tonight, so if you need to get a hold of me you will know where to find me. I think in the morning, we need to have a nice long talk about what direction the family needs to be heading."

"Sounds good boss." Sledge, Drift's old right-hand man says before he smacks me on the back and nods as his greying dark brown hair shifts to the side with the movement.

I don't know why I still command such respect from everyone, but for the most part they all seem to still want to follow me. And that is good. On the other hand, there are one or two strays like Crow and Buzz who don't from what I see and that will be a problem I may have to deal with first thing in the morning.

"Ready?" I ask when I turn to Amy and take Jonathan into my arms.

"Yeah, just follow behind me. I moved last year when we started to have trouble on the edge of town. Now I live in the center. It is more peaceful there. Especially, with Jonathan here." She murmurs as she walks towards her small blue sedan.

Somehow, I had completely missed it as I walked up to everyone. But as soon as I open the door with my left hand and expertly cradle Jonathan with the other, she scoops him up in her arms. After she puts him in his baby seat, she turns to me and hugs me tight.

"I don't know what I would do without you here." She says before a stray tear escapes the corner of her eye.

"Amy don't worry about it. You have always been like a big sis to me. Family is family and I should have never left you all behind. It was selfish of me, and I will be the first to admit that I was wrong for doing it. I really hate myself sometimes for doing so." I reply sadly as I think about what would have happened if I had been the leader at the time.

I would be the one in the casket right now, not Drift. Perhaps it would have been for the best considering the baby and all. But I can't help but wonder if it had to have happened at all. Or if we could have prevented it if we had just gone straight sooner.

"Don't beat yourself up. We all still love you and you will always be the leader in all our eyes. Everyone knows I loved Drift, but he was weak compared to you. He did not know how to run a business and stay out of trouble." she says softly as she opens the door and sits down.

As soon as she shuts the door, I hurry back to my bike and quickly put on my helmet and my skull face mask. While I sit there, I watch her pull out of the line of bikes and then drive past me slowly. Her eyes are filled with sadness as she waits for me to follow behind her.

By the time we get back to her house it is getting dark out. So, I quickly pull in behind her car in the driveway. Then I look at the little yellow house staring back at me. It suits her needs for all intents and purposes, but you would never catch me living here if I could help it.

It's just too white-picket fence for me. Honestly, I don't know how Drift could have stood to live here either. After all, we grew up in a shitty little single wide trailer home in the trailer park. That was all we needed.

"Come on." She states with sadness in her eyes after she gets Jonathan and her purse out of the car.

However, when she goes to unlock the house and the door is ajar, I stop her quickly and push her to the side. I put my finger to my lips to shush her and wave her to get back. Then I cautiously open the door to reveal a big mess.

"What the fuck?" I say in worry as I look around the room and realize that they could still be around waiting for us to return.

I rush back out to find her standing where I had left her. No worse for wear. Good thing or I might have to kill someone tonight. Not what I had wanted to happen the first night back in town, but I knew it was always a possibility.

"Come on. Stand behind me and we will go through each room. I don't feel comfortable with you standing out here in the open." I say in alarm as I start to feel something is wrong.

I am just really glad that I grabbed my trusty gun out of my bag before heading on in.

Once we go through every room, I begin to calm down a little bit until I notice the letter on the fridge. It's in Drift's handwriting and it says, "I will be home late tonight. We have something I must take care of first."

As soon as I realized that this must have been the last thing he did before he went and died that night, it began to creep me out. Especially, knowing that he knew there was a chance he might not make it back. There always was.

"What's wrong?" she asks worriedly after she puts Jonathan in his crib and tucks him in for a nap.

"Nothing. Just leave me alone right now. I need to figure this out. Clearly, they were sending a message. But what they don't realize is they are fucking with my family now and I don't put up with nobody's shit." I growl as I turn on my heels and walk out of the room.

After sitting down on the old brown leather couch, I pull out my phone and dial a number I thought I would never use again. Rider has always been the one to put someone down when we needed a quick fix and no mess on our hands. He was reliable and didn't give a shit who he had to kill because it was just business as usual to him.

When I hear breathing on the other end, I quickly say, "I need a problem taken care of, but I don't know who yet. Can you get here say tomorrow morning? Then I will lay out the details."

I hear a gruff voice reply, "Yeah, 11?"

"Of course. That will work. Just meet me at the usual." I reply cautiously while being very aware that anyone could be listening in on our conversation.

"Sure." He states before hanging up.

With that out of the way, I slouch down on the couch and then hear a knock at the door. I immediately stand and instinctively put my hand to my back pocket to where my gun is. I can't help it because for years I carried a gun wherever I went.

"Who is it?" I bark at the person on the other side of the door as I walk quickly over to it and stand to the side.

"Trixie." A woman's voice says as she replies seductively.

"Come on. Let me in. This is Kim. Don't you remember us? We just want to have some fun." She says as she laughs and knocks again.

I cautiously unlock the door and open it an inch to see two girls in their late 20's wearing barely anything, standing at the door. They seem more than a little drunk as they caress each other. Yeah, those were the good old days when I never went to bed alone. Often with two or three sucking my dick and eating each other out.

Because I didn't see any harm in it, I open the door and let them in before I lock it again. Right away, Trixie runs her slender fingers up my inner leg right to my balls, then she digs her nails in before Kim takes my hand seductively and leads me to the couch with a shake of her ass.

She pushes me down and then drops to her knees before she begins to unzip my pants. "Fuck. You two are hot." I say as my dick hardens instantly and starts to throb.

"Who was it?" Amy asks quietly as she walks in on us, then quickly leaves the room the moment she looks at the girls and sees what is going on.

She knows better than to interrupt this. I bet there were many nights that Drift did the same thing. It is just our way, and she knows it. Even if she was married to him, it didn't change the fact that we usually don't ever stay with one woman. Ever. Life is too short to be tied down to one person.

## Chapter 6: Life Is Good

"I want to watch the two of you touch each other first!" I exclaim louder than I should have as my cock jerks to attention.

"Lose those clothes. After all, I rather enjoyed watching you caress her nice big tits. Then tease and suck them for me." I demand in a deep voice as my heart begins to beat faster now.

What I really want is to watch them eat each other out as I sit back and enjoy myself. God that gets me so hard it isn't funny. Especially, when they know I am watching their every move. But for the time being, I think I will wait to see just how far they will go without too much prompting.

"Like this…" Trixie says breathlessly as she slips her top off and then circles her perfectly pink and perky nipples deliberately with the tip of her middle finger.

A moment later, she licks her lips and flicks her long, straight blonde hair out of the way as she watches Kim strip down almost immediately to nothing but her hot pink thong. Then she giggles and says so softly I can barely hear her, "Yummy. I want you to sit on my face because I love it when you are about to cum, and you suffocate me with your legs."

"Fuck. The two of you are already making my balls ache. Now get to it. Bitch, grab a mouthful of that titty and suck it for me."

Trixie obeys my command as she licks her lips once again and firmly grasps Kim's left breast. As she leans down to lick the pebbled dark pink nipple, she makes a soft moaning sound and closes her eyes before she takes a large portion of it in her mouth. While she continues to suck, her other hand slinks down to Kim's clit.

As her hand lowers down, she slips it into Kim's thong slowly, and I watch as Kim's eyes flutter shut. She throws her head back and a faint moan escapes her lips before I hear Trixie's finger slide in and out. It makes a sucking sound like when you suck on a lollipop, but much wetter.

While I watch the two of them go at it, I deny myself the pleasure of stroking him for at least the moment because I need to save all my strength for when I get to fuck them both. After all, it has been a very long day, and I am admittedly a bit tired. Plus, there is the fact that before this I had been restricting myself to one woman.

"Rip those panties off for me, Trixie. I want to see if she is shaved or not." I demand as I grow hungrier and hungrier for them.

She turns to look at me and then says slyly, "Your wish is my command." Before she withdraws her finger and rips it off in one movement.

"Yes, yes she is." I think to myself as I gaze down at her pubic region and admire the freshly shaven area.

Kim stares at me for a second to wait for approval so I nod before she returns her gaze to Trixie and cups her chin. She asks her hesitantly in a breathless voice, "Please, will you keep going? I need you."

She looks at me for approval once again, and when I nod with a smile, she drops to her knees and takes both Kim's hands. "Lay down on the couch, I want to lick that sweet honey pot."

After Kim lays down next to me, I watch as Trixie positions herself perfectly between Kim's slender long legs and lowers her head. Then begins to lick her soaked folds agonizingly slowly. "Mm. Tastes so sweet. Just like I remember." She remarks as she looks up at me before she slides two fingers in her wet pussy and rubs her clit with her thumb.

"Uh, uh. If you keep that up, I am going to cum in no time." Kim admits breathlessly as she wraps her fingers around Trixie's hair and forces her face right between her legs again. She tights around her neck as Trixie begins to lick her nub lightly.

"Fuck….. fuck me with two more fingers. I need to feel you. Faster." She says in between breaths as I watch Trixie eat her out voraciously.

Trixie licks her nub one more time and inserts the other two fingers before Kim cries out and squirts all over her face. It is amazing because she seems to keep squirting for over a minute as she cries out and keeps a tight hold on Trixie's head. When I can't handle it anymore, I take advantage of the situation by getting behind Trixie and discovering that she has no panties on under her miniskirt.

As I get a bird's eye view of her pussy, I decide which entrance I want to go in first.

But first things first. Before I ever touch these girls, I need to put on protection because God only knows who has fucked them before me. So, I quickly pull out my wallet and find a condom.

After I slide my pants down, I slip it on easily because I am already rock-hard. As I feel the warmth of my palm touch it, I shudder and then I run my fingers over him tightly. Without warning I dig my fingers into Trixie's hips before I thrust him in her wet pussy hard and fast. She tightens around me instantly and begins to moan as I quickly fill her hot little cunt.

At first, I go fast for a few quick thrusts, but then I slow clear down to make her beg. When she doesn't, I all together stop and withdraw quickly before I hear her cry out, "But why? I need you."

I hesitate while my dick hovers just an inch from her ass and then I rub it on her rim in a circle slowly. "How bad do you need him, slut?"

"Angel, please. I need him so bad it hurts." She begs as she thrusts her butt towards me.

I take that as a yes and slam him deep in her. She cries out as I stretch her to the limits and begin to bury him in her long and hard. Within just a few minutes, I can already start to feel her begin to loosen for me as she whimpers in pain. I can't help but to smirk because she is just another one of the whores who like to hang out with the gang, hoping for their next score.

"Chicks like this are a dime a dozen and when you use them you throw them out like the garbage they are." Drift often said before he met Amy, and then suddenly he changed his mind.

All the gang felt this way about the women who hung on our every word. Biker chicks come and go, but our family is what really counts. I should have remembered that, but for some reason I forgot it the moment my brother was killed.

When Trixie turns around and gazes at me in need a flash of a raven-haired beauty pops in my head. Right away, I try to shake the memory away and pound harder as I fuck her brains out.

"Angel, I am going to cum. Oh, Angel." Trixie cries out before Kim kisses her full on the mouth and her finger finds Trixie's folds.

When Kim begins to rub her, Trixie loses it and comes hard. She tightens around my swollen cock and as soon as she does, I fill the condom completely. Then I quickly withdraw, so I don't accidentally lose it in her. Because honestly, the last thing I need is for one of these dumb bitches to get pregnant with my kid.

"I will be right back. I want you two to gobble me down before you leave." I say gruffly as I stand up and find the bathroom.

Once I throw away the condom and wash him off, I return to see that they are kissing each other passionately. Upon further inspection, I notice that Kim's fingers are buried in Trixie's pussy and her other hand is teasing her hard nipple.

"Hey, you two. Get over here and suck my dick. You have some gobbling to do." I state shortly as I sit down on the couch in front of them and stroke him a few times.

Kim kneels before me, and Trixie sits next to me on the couch as they eye him up. First, Kim leans down and takes him in both hands. She strokes him once and then lowers her head.

Just as soon as her warm lips touch the head, my eyes roll back, and a deep moan escapes my lips. They feel like silk as he slides in, and she begins to deep throat him. In and out, in and out, then she licks him in a circle with the tip of her tongue.

"Fuck. You are a professional, aren't you?" I ask as I throw my head back and feel my balls become heavy.

She stops and I open my eyes to watch Trixie kiss her and lick the precum off Kim's lips. Then as Kim's long dark brown hair cascades over him, it tickles. But a second later she makes it all better by deep throating him again.

As she does, I watch Trixie lean down and suck my balls hard. She nips at them and then takes them both in her mouth and sucks harder. If they keep this up, I am going to burst quickly.

When I realize this, I wrap my fingers around Kim's soft hair and hold her down, so she stays on him. As she chokes and coughs, a smirk spreads across my face and I eventually let her up. She gasps for air and that is when I notice the tears in her eyes.

"Could she really not breathe?" I wonder to myself as I thrust her back down on him and force her to start to choke again. Well, good. I like it when they struggle.

Trixie bites down on my balls playfully and when she does, I groan and then cum so hard it feels as if the earth shakes. I feel a spasm go up my spine and then I blow my wad inside Trixie's mouth.

She begins to choke and gag even louder now but I won't let go of her head and force her to stay exactly where she is. "Suck it cunt. Lick it clean for me. After all, you know you want to eat that shit like a good little whore and maybe later on I will fill all of your holes too." I say matter-of-factly before I eventually let go of her head and she comes up for air.

The moment she looks at me, I see fear in her eyes. Does she think I would have choked her to death? Hm. Maybe. But not likely because she isn't worth the trouble it would cause me.

Then as I glance over at Kim, I see that raven haired girl again. Fuck her. I don't need this right now.

"Get out of here. I am done with you two for the moment. Right now, I just need some sleep." I bark as I stand up and wave the two of them out.

They quickly grab their clothes and put them on before they rush out the door, just barely getting their shoes back on. Then I lock it behind them and murmur under my breath, "Good, now I can finally get some sleep."

Of course, I could be wrong because the moment the door slams shut, the baby wakes up and he won't stop crying.

## Chapter 7: Really Early The Next Morning

It takes all night to calm the little one down or at least it feels like it because we take turns holding and rocking him for a large part of the night. That is until he finally goes to sleep.

"I think he is teething." Amy whispers as she walks towards the door and shuts off the light.

I follow her and then shut the door behind me while still leaving it open just a crack. When I glance at her face, I notice how tired she looks. I instantly feel a twinge of guilt eat at me because she should never have had to go through this alone. It was all my fault and I know it to be the truth. But right now, I just want to close my eyelids and sleep like the dead before the sun comes up and I must face what is coming.

"I am heading to bed Amy. I might suggest you try to get some sleep too before he wakes up again." I say hesitantly because I know better than that.

"I can't. I still have the laundry to get done and to make his formula. But get some sleep. There is no doubt that you will have a busy morning trying to rein everyone back in." She whispers as she rubs the back of her neck and her shoulder.

Because I realized that she was right I nodded, and then headed off to the spare bedroom. As soon as I open the door, I note that it is quite small, but there is a light blue waterfront scene on the wallpaper that seems to make it feel bigger somehow. Not to mention, there is a big bay window that looks over her petite little rose garden.

"How cozy." I murmur under my breath sarcastically before I sit down on the bed and kick off my dress shoes.

I have been in this suit for far too long and now it is time to become comfortable in just my own skin. After all, I prefer to sleep that way. I always have. However, when I hear a quick little unexpected knock, I sigh and ask quietly, "What's up?"

"I just wanted to make sure you have everything you need." She says softly so she doesn't wake the baby.

I smirk and then reply jokingly, "Well, yes but if you had waited just a minute or two longer, you might have gotten an eyeful, and I don't know if you would have welcomed that."

There is an uncomfortable silence as she clearly is thinking about this. I wonder. Suddenly it occurs to me that even though she has always thought of me as a little brother, she might want me to fill the void that Drift left.

I mean I wouldn't say no, but it would be a little awkward. Especially, if she became my woman and she got pregnant again. That would be a whole other story. As a matter of fact, just thinking about it gives me a bad taste in my mouth as I wipe my hands on my pant legs.

"You do know I was just joking right?" I ask but when I don't hear an answer, I open the door.

When I look down at her, she is leaning up against the door frame with a far off look in her eyes and for the first time I notice that her blonde hair is pulled up. The look is one of need and that ache is one only a hard cock can fill. She wants it alright, but I can't bring myself to do it.

"Amy." I murmur quietly as I stare down at her.

She quickly glances up at me with shame on her face and then rushes off to her bedroom. I can only assume she will take care of business her own way because I am not naïve enough to think that all women don't have play toys hiding under their beds for times just like this. After all, women have needs just like men do.

By the time I sit back down on the edge of the bed, I start to see the faint glimmer of sunrise appear over the buildings.

"Shit." I say a little too loudly before I hush myself and then murmur, "Fuck."

Of course, I couldn't sleep just a few hours. No. Instead, I am going to be mad as sin all day now. What a way to start the day.

I shake my head and then stand up before I run my hand over my stubble and sigh loudly. I guess it could be worse. At least, I have Rider coming into town later this morning to take care of my problem.

When I realized that I still needed to identify the culprit, I put in a call to action by dialing Sledge's number and waking him up.

"Sorry Sledge. I need you to get everyone to the club house so we can discuss a few things." I say flatly as I stare out the window and wonder what to do first.

"Sure thing. Did you even get any sleep last night? I know I sent over Trixie and Kim because they wanted to cheer you up." He says jokingly as he yawns and then I hear a woman's voice in the background.

"Not really. After I kicked them out, little Jonathan decided to wake up and cry the rest of the night." I reply slowly as I stretch and walk to my bag so I can change out of this suit.

"Anyway, I need to take a piss and get some coffee in me. I will see you in about an hour. Sound good?" I ask as I pull out a pair of jeans and a short-sleeved black T-shirt.

"Yep, just let me kick this bitch out and I will be right on it." He says gruffly before he hangs up.

After placing the phone on the bed, I quickly change and then do my deeds in the bathroom. As soon as I walk out, I hear Jonathan crying again so I open the door and see Amy practically sleepwalking with him in her arms.

"Come here you little rugrat." I murmur as I take him from her and notice that he has a full diaper.

"Let's get that little stinky butt changed before it explodes all over your poor mom." I murmur under my breath while smiling at him.

I can't help it. He is so adorable, and it is so hard to believe that he is my nephew.

"Did he wake you?" Amy asks softly while yawning and stretching.

She walks over to the changing table as I wipe his little butt clean. Then I turn to her and reply sweetly, "Nah, I never went to sleep. I have things to do this morning that can't wait."

I pause as a flash of that mystery girl pops back in my head and I hesitate to ask, but eventually I cautiously do, "Say, you wouldn't happen to know anything else about the daughter of The Devils Legion, would you? You know that girl we saw at the cemetery, and you said to stay away from her."

She closes her eyes for a second and then shakes her head before she answers me bitterly, "I know that she is nothing but trouble. She is beautiful, but she isn't worth it. They never are. All she will do is be the end of you when her daddy finds out. Don't you know that her daddy is the one who killed Drift? While Drift and a few of the boys were up by the cliffs doing a drug deal, his gang rode by and shot him dead.

Honestly, I think it was a set up to get rid of him and run us all out of town."

"That I didn't know, and I am sorry. It was on my list of things to find out. I am glad you told me but now I know what I must do." I reply softly as I stare at Jonathan and hope that I can keep him safe and out of the way of harm.

"Fuck them all. They will wish that I had never came back to town when this is all said and done." I murmur under my breath before I hand him off to her and turn around to walk out the door.

## Chapter 8: Justine's Sleepless Night

After getting completely stuffed, I start to fall asleep in the living room, so grandma jabs me gently and then says so sweetly, "Go to bed. We can finish the movie tomorrow night. I bet you have had such a long day."

I nod, and then stand up before grandpa smiles and adds, "Don't forget that tomorrow I need you to head to town and fetch me a new saw. This one finally died."

"No problem grandpa. I need to get a few things anyways while I am in town." I reply as I start to walk to my room slowly.

I guess I never realized just how much it takes out of me when I go see mom. But what I can't get out of my head is the image of that man. He haunted me all throughout dinner. In my dream he started to ask me something before grandma woke me up.

I need to know more about him. Why was he there at the funeral for The Road Rangers MC's leader? Is he one of them? God, I certainly hope not because that means he is my dad's enemy, and all of them end up dead eventually by his hand or others.

When I reach my bedroom, I glance around at the small, but cozy room with tan painted walls and a four-post wooden bed in the middle of the room. It is sparsely decorated because I like it that way and I have never cared for that cluttered look anyways. Besides, I really don't require much to be happy, just as long as I have people who love me and a place to lay my head at night.

Once I grab my silky white nightgown out of the drawer, I take off my shirt and pants before I pull it over my head. It always feels so good as it slides over my skin and reminds me of a man's fingers as they caress me slowly. "Mm." I moan while imagining that man running his fingers over my skin as soft as a feather.

I might just have to pull out my vibrator and enjoy myself a little before I can go to sleep. After all, visions of him bending me over the bed from behind begin to cloud my judgement as I walk over to the closet and pull out an old black shoe box. It contains my most prized possession, a bright red vibrator with a butt plug attachment. I remember back to many a night that I laid in bed while imagining myself getting fucked by two men filling me completely.

"Now for some music to set the mood." I murmur under my breath as I turn on the CD player and my favorite music starts to play.

When I turn around, I sit down on the bed and slide under the covers with my toy in hand. I close my eyes and twist the base before it starts to whir to life. "Mm." I whisper breathlessly as I recall the exact look on his face.

What I wouldn't do to have him fill me right now. I don't even care if he is my family's enemy. If he feels as good as he looks, I couldn't care in the least bit.

As I slide the tip over my nub, I shudder and begin to moan softly. However, when I slide him in and he fills both, I fight to keep quiet. It feels so good when it tickles me as I thrust it in and out. And when I hold it in place at just the right angle, I begin to feel my orgasm build, my clit throb for more.

So, I throw my head back and begin to breathe heavily as I slip it in and out, faster and faster. I see his face before he turns me around and spreads me wide. Right before he does, I look down to see his gigantic cock and it is as hard as a rock for me as he demands in a deep voice, "Scream for me. I am going to fuck you so hard baby that you will dream about me every time you close those gorgeous eyes."

Just as soon as he says it, he smacks my ass and I squeal in delight because that is just one of my weaknesses. Of course, there is always more. For one thing, I like to be choked and another I love to use my man's dick as a pacifier to sleep at night. There is just something about a man's dick in my mouth that calms me right down.

The moment I think about his big dick in my mouth, I hit my special spot and let out a loud "uh" as I cum harder than I ever have with any man. Then my pussy squeezes it tight, and I see a million brightly colored stars under my eyelids. After realizing that my grandparents could have heard me, I work through my orgasm quickly. Then I lay there for a few minutes before I managed to jump up and return my play toy to its spot in the closet out of prying eyes. The whole time my nub throbs for more as I slide back under the silky covers.

"Now, maybe I can finally get some sleep." I murmur sleepily as visions of my mystery man pop back into my head.

As I begin to wonder who he is, I decide I won't be able to sleep until I touch myself one last time. When I run my forefinger over my overly sensitive soaked folds, I begin to moan and lick my lips. With my other hand, I pinch my hard left nipple and tug on it, so it hurts. Then I thrust two fingers in my slit.

I almost cry out, but don't when I slide in the other two and feel completely full. Of course, I could have gotten my toy back out, but there is something to say for the feel of skin on skin. It feels so good, and the warmth is irreplaceable.

While I rub my clit with my thumb, I slide the four fingers in and out rapidly. Then I feel it become so slick with my juices that they slip in and out easily now. "Fuck." I murmur under my breath as I bite my lip and wish that the mystery man was here to finish the job the good old-fashioned way.

But because he is not, I slide my fingers in and out several more times as I twirl them around inside me like an erotic dance between two lovers. No more than a second later, I tighten around them and feel the orgasm grip me from head to toe. As my body jerks involuntarily, I bite my lip again and this time I sense the taste of copper before I realize that there is blood on my tongue.

Just as soon as I calm down and my breathing returns to normal, I get up and walk to the bathroom to grab a washcloth before cleaning up.

Afterwards, I stare in the mirror at my reflection and wonder what men really see in me. Is it my big breasts? My slender body? Or something else? As I continue to stare, I wonder if he thinks about me as much as I do him because I can't allow myself to get close. Not even for an instant.

As soon as I realized that I had left the hot water on, I shut it off and walked back into the bedroom. Then after I looked around the room one last time, I finally lay my head down on the pillow and fall fast asleep with a dirty little smile on my lips. For the moment I am fully satisfied.

## Chapter 9: Plotting Revenge

I already know what I must do. From the moment I get on my bike, it is clear as day now that I must put an end to their leader for sure.

"I will get my revenge if it is the last thing I do." I murmur under my breath angrily and speed off.

A few minutes later as I drive up to the stop light and look around, I lay eyes on a woman standing on the street corner. Too late do I realize that it is Brick's daughter. As she crosses the street, I start to think that getting my revenge may be harder than I initially thought it would be. Especially, if I can't stop thinking with my dick.

After she gets to the other side, she pauses at the corner and looks directly at me. I know that she feels this strange connection too and that troubles me more than anything. However, when she stares into my eyes, I feel like she is peering into my soul, and I can't help but not want to claim her right then and there as mine.

The daughter of my enemy is staring at me as if she is thinking the same thing. "I wonder." I murmur under my breath before she finally turns away and begins to walk to her destination.

Because I am not paying attention, I miss the change of the lights and I don't budge an inch. Then the car behind me honks and the man yells out his window angrily, "Move that piece of shit out of the way."

My head whips around as I hear him state it. Instantly, I yell snidely, "Excuse me? What did I just hear you say?"

The man in the car hurriedly rolls up his window as I get off my bike and push the kick stand out. The next thing I know, I flip him off and rush towards the vehicle without ever thinking about the consequences of my actions.

"Can you say that a little louder? I don't think I heard you." I demand when he doesn't say another word.

I am itching for a fight this morning and it might as well start right here. Especially, knowing that I have had no sleep, and my nerves are getting worn.

"Well?" I ask while getting more and more agitated with every second the man sits there silently.

Now when I look down at him from where I stand, he appears scared as I watch him fumble for his phone to call for help.

"Oh, come on. Fucker, are you actually going to call the police?" I ask snidely because I already know far too well that is exactly what he aims to do.

So, I slam my palms against his window and say loudly, "Come on."

But before I ever get a chance to scare the shit out of him, a tall, thin cop pulls up next to me and asks in an authoritative voice, "Do we have a problem here, buddy?"

He stares at me impatiently and then up at the green light before asking again, "Do we have a problem here? Or will you get back on your bike and drive? I don't need any more problems here. We already have enough of our own."

"I guess you don't recognize me then." I reply sarcastically before I take off the mask and my smile spreads from ear to ear.

Tony should remember me from high school but then again it has been several years since he has seen me around here. When he doesn't seem to recognize me at first, I take out my wallet and produce three crisp one hundred-dollar bills. I fold them and then offer the bundle to him before I say quietly so no one else hears, "I suggest you forget about it and let me go about my business."

He looks down at the money and then back at me before he seems to realize who I am. "Oh, man. For a moment there I thought I was going to have to run you in." he says happily. "How long has it been?" he asks before he turns to the car and waves it around us.

"Not long enough." I reply under my breath as I watch him wave traffic through and then return his attention to me.

"Say, will you be in town for long? I wouldn't mind getting a drink with you after work tonight."

"I am afraid I might be staying. My brother Drift's funeral was yesterday and now I am the head of the Road Rangers again." I state sadly as I watch traffic drive by.

"Yeah, I worked on the files. The attorney's office ruled that it was a clear case of a drug deal. The Devil's Legion was to blame but we couldn't find anything that would stick so we had to let them go for the time being."

He says sadly as he furrows his brow and frowns at the ground.

"But hey, at least you are back, and we can play catch up tonight." He adds while turning his frown into a smile as he looks at the oncoming traffic.

"No problem. What time do you get out?" I ask softly as I watch a familiar face drive by.

"8 p.m. Do you want to meet up at The Den?" he replies quickly before his radio starts to make loud chattering sounds.

"Tony, pick up. We have trouble at the gas station. Some guy just drove off without paying for his gas." An older woman's voice says sternly before he takes the radio out of its holder.

"Alright. I was checking on a traffic jam, but the situation has cleared up and I am just down the road so I will be there in a few minutes." He says as he smiles at me and then starts to walk back to his car before he stops suddenly.

"See you then." He adds before getting in and driving off as I put my mask back on and get back on my bike.

I follow him to the next road. Afterwards, I turn left and head to the club house while trying to decide what I am going to do about this whole thing. First, I think I will get the background information on the head of the Devils Legion. Hopefully, it might help us get a leg ahead. Then and only then I will fill in Rider on all the details.

After all, I have come to the realization that if I don't kill him myself, I won't ever truly feel that Drift has been avenged. I must see it in his eyes. But I can use Rider to get rid of his right-hand man and anyone else who might get in the way. Even if that includes his daughter.

## Chapter 10: The Clubhouse

Once I see the lights on at the club, I feel reassured that everything is going as planned and park my bike by the entrance.

"Hey, look who's here?" I hear a familiar male voice announce as I look around to see Snake slither up to the side of me.

He was so named Snake because he had this way about him that just didn't seem normal. As he walks, he makes no noise unless he wants you to hear him.

"Hey, I guess you got the call. Is everyone else here?" I ask as I scan the area for the other bikes.

"Mm. Yeah. Although they are a little pissed that they had to get up so damn early this morning. You must have had something really important for us all in order to get us up at the butt fuck crack of dawn like this. As a matter of fact, I was just about to go to bed when the phone rang."

"I am sorry about that, but I think it is important that we take care of our little problem before anyone else ends up dead. And then there is the fact that I have Rider heading in this morning and he needs to know who to get rid of before he will do anything." I reply softly so no one else can hear but the two of us.

"Oh, fuck. Are you planning on taking over their area too then?" he asks curiously before he points at a couple of bikers walking in.

"Yes, I think it's necessary if we are going to go legit. I mean, this place has been a drug haven since we all moved in, and I think it is about time we cleaned it up so my nephew can grow up safer. We owe it to Drift and Amy to do that for them. Of course, we will still run guns, but it will be mostly on the up and up through legal channels. Now, who is to say that we won't do a few sales on the side, but the trick is to not get caught doing it."

"Is this shit show going to start or are we going to hang out and play poker all morning?" I hear a hungover Trouble yell from the door as he pokes his head out and flips me off.

I nod, before Snake and I walk in. As I shut the door behind us, I take inventory of everyone when I notice that Crow and Buzz are back. I honestly did not think they would show up this morning but when they did, to tell you the truth I was pleased.

"So, I called you all here this morning because we have a problem and I think you all know what and who I am referring to. Brick and The Devils Legion need to disappear. I have a few thoughts on that but right now I would like to know all the information you have on their whereabouts and families. If necessary, we will go after the families but only if they pose a threat to ours. In the meantime, I need you all to keep a close look out for anything suspicious because I do expect retaliation once I take out Brick and his right-hand man." I announce authoritatively and then sit down at the table to listen to what they all have to say.

No more than a second later, I hear a knock at the door and everyone's attention is drawn to it. I quickly walk over, but before I dare open it, I stand to the side and ask, "Who is it?" loudly.

"Who the fuck do you think it is?" I hear Rider say snidely before he shoves the door open and gives me a big smile.

"I wish I could say that I was here under other circumstances, but it is what it is." He adds before giving me a hug and walking in without hesitation.

Rider is nearly a good foot shorter than I am, so I am forced to look down at him when he speaks.

"You are early." I reply sarcastically before shutting the door and returning my attention to the room.

"Yeah, well I figured the sooner the better. So, what info do you have for me?"

"That is exactly what I was trying to work out before you arrived. So, instead, why don't you take a seat, and we will find out together." I suggest as I point to the vacant leather chair next to mine.

"Hey, by the way, does anyone know where Sledge is?" I ask worriedly when I realize that he isn't here yet.

Everyone looks around and begins to shake their heads before their phones ring simultaneously. Then with a frown, I watch as Snake puts his phone on speaker, and I hear Tony's voice say hesitantly, "Snake, Sledge's body was just found up at Dead Man's Curve. As a matter of fact, his body was still warm when I arrived on the scene just a few minutes ago. The worst part of it all is the fact that no one saw it happen."

As we sit quietly in shock, everyone else reads the text about it on their phones. Then we all sink in our chairs and realize that it could have been any one of us. Something must be done now.

"Thanks, buddy. Let me know if you hear anything." Snake murmurs into the phone before putting it back in his pocket and staring at me with hatred in his eyes.

"Let's kill them all." He says angrily as he stares at me and then looks at the others.

I wait patiently and sit back as I watch everyone before I finally announce, "This is what we are going to do. I have hired Rider to get rid of Brick's right-hand man and then while it is mass chaos over there, I will kill Brick and make him pay for them. I must see the terror in his eyes when he realizes that he is about to die. Once they are both dead, we will pick the rest of them off one by one so they can see how it feels. That is how we will get our ultimate revenge for Sledge and Drift. At this point I don't care if the women and children are caught in the crossfire. They all need to pay." I spit vehemently as I narrow my eyes and glance at each one of them.

"Now, as I said before. Does anyone have information that will help us?"

A few of them murmur in the background and then Hawk stands up and growls hatefully while he runs his fingers through his long blonde hair, "I think I might know where to find them this morning. They have been hanging out by the beachfront at the old diner Milly's."

A second later, Tiny stands up and slams his fist into the table, making a loud crashing sound before he yells, "Then let's go fucking get them."

After standing up quickly, I yell loudly over everyone, "No, we need to follow the plan.

Once we do that, the rest of them will be easy to pick off one by one. But with their leader in place, they are stronger because their gang is bigger than ours."

Suddenly, everyone quiets down and then Rider stands up next to me while stating, "It makes sense. Just let me know where I need to go, and I will get it done before any more of you get killed."

"Of course, I had already planned on it. Now, does anyone know for sure where Brick and Gear are? Has anyone seen them?" I ask as I stare at each member intently before moving onto the next because our very lives may depend on their answers.

When I stop at Austin, I watch as he furrows his brow and hesitates to look at me. Finally, a moment later he stares up into my eyes and answers quietly, "I saw Gear this morning at Tonya's house. Apparently, she has decided to switch sides."

"Well, I guess we have our answer then. No wonder why they seem to always know where we are going to be." I say as I turn to Rider and frown at him before I add hesitantly, "You know where Gear will be. I don't care how you do it, but get it done now. I don't want any more bloodshed on my hands, but this is necessary for the survival of our club."

He nods, and then murmurs under his breath, "Understood." Before he heads for the door.

Just before he walks out, I notice the Beretta in his back pocket and already know that he will finish the job without any problems.

## Chapter 11: The Games That We Play

When business has been completed the women are allowed into the meeting room for a few minutes before we head out. Sara and Monica bring several bottles of whiskey with them as they slink around in their black leather microskirts and skimpy sleeveless t-shirts that are so tight you can see their nipples pebbling under the thin fabric. Monica takes a seat on the edge of the table directly in front of me before she leans down and cascades her straggly long bleach blonde hair over my lap.

At first, everyone sits down and just watches as the girls begin to amuse themselves, but then Sara takes a seat next to her before running her fingertips over her breasts. She then leans over and licks her lips before she slips her left hand under Monica's shirt and sighs softly.

"Fuck, you two sure know how to quiet a room and get everyone's attention. But I want to see more than touching." I say before I lean in so close, I can feel their breath on my face and I add in a whisper, "Eat each other out real slow. I want to see the ecstasy on your faces as you cum in each other's mouths."

Sara nods with a grin before she hikes her skirt up quickly and climbs on Monica. As she positions herself over her face, I sit back and watch the show. A few seconds later, she slowly lowers down onto her before I hear sucking sounds and muffled moans from Sara's mouth.

Suddenly, inspiration strikes so I withdraw my weapon from my back pocket and slide forward in the chair. Then when Sara lifts a little, I rub the cold metal of the muzzle on her rim. I smile when I find out that it is already slippery from her juices, so I slide it effortlessly into her tight little ass.

Right away she cries out as she lifts her head and stares back at me for a second angrily in between moans of pure ecstasy. Then she whimpers as Monica bites down on her clit and she inserts two fingers in her. When she loosens her grip on the muzzle, I begin to slide it in and out slowly. Teasing her with it as she tightens her ass around it.

"Man, that is so fucking hot." Buzz says as he stands up and walks over to where I am sitting before adding, "I like the view over here much better."

I nod to him but keep one eye on the girls as I slip the gun in and out, then Buzz moves closer and bumps into me as he watches them, so I stop for a second. As I glance up at him and wonder just how close he needs to be, Sara slams her ass into my hand. What she doesn't realize is that it is fully loaded and could go off in her at any second if I accidentally pull the trigger. So, when she takes it like a pro, I reward her by filling her harder until I hear her cry out and I watch as she shudders uncontrollably.

When I can't take it any longer, I pull the gun slowly out of her ass, place it on the table in front of me and then stand as I unzip my pants.

"That's my good girls." I say in praise as I make up my mind what I want to do with them. Fill them or let them get down on their knees and worship me? So many options. Meanwhile, the other guys don't even argue while this is happening because they know that their turn will come soon enough.

"You guys are so very hot together. Do you know that? But I want to see what the two of you do with this." I say as I dry stroke him from the tip to the base slowly with a tight fist, then I raise my hand to Sara's bottom lip before I rub my thumb over it softly.

She smiles and then I force my thumb into her mouth, but she starts to gag when I hold her tongue down. "Now do be a good girl and make sure to relax while I fuck your face. I don't need anyone biting down when you start to choke." I say loudly as the guys watch every movement I make.

"You can still do that right? I know it has been years since you have taken him in your mouth, but I think you can handle it."

Sara nods, and then sucks on my thumb before I slip it out and watch the spit slide out of her mouth. As she drops to her knees, Monica takes her place next to her and looks up at me. Her eyes are instantly wide as she runs her fingers up my inner thighs and works my aching balls through my jeans.

"Here let me get that for you." I say as I pull my jeans down and my cock springs back up to attention.

As soon as I do, Monica's fingers find my balls as she begins to squeeze them tightly while Sara digs her fingers into my ass and wraps her lips around my tip. When I feel the warmth surrounding it, I throw my head back and close my eyes because I can't take it anymore. It feels so good.

"Damn it." I cry out as I start to feel my orgasm build quickly.

Of course, right at that moment an image of my raven-haired beauty pops in my head as I bend her over and fuck her senseless.

"I am going to cum soon!" I yell before grabbing a handful of Monica's hair and yanking on it.

She whimpers and then squeezes my balls tighter as I fuck Sara's face and use her as my cock sleeve. But when I imagine "her" in place of Sara, I can't hold it anymore and explode full force down her throat. She begins to choke and then gag as my thick seed slides down. But the moment I am done, I lick my lips slowly and open my eyes to see everyone staring at us.

While I continue to look around, I look down at the two of them and I realize that I am still pulling Monica's hair. So, I quickly release it and watch as Sara wipes her mouth before getting up.

"Do you mind if I take a turn?" Trouble asks cautiously as he walks over and offers a hand to Monica.

I hesitate for a second and then shake my head before he bends her over the table and unzips his pants. Soon after Buzz picks up Sara and carries her over to his chair before he takes a seat and has her sit on his lap.

"You are so wet." He murmurs just barely loud enough for me to hear before he thrusts hard into her and begins to help her move up and down on him.

As I watch intently, I step back to sit down in my chair so I can see the show unfold in front of me. But before I can even get comfortable with my dick in my hand, my phone rings and I realize that it is Rider. For a second, I hesitate to answer it, even though I know that it is important. However, eventually I answer it and then he says quietly, "I am outside of Tonya's place. I watched gear leave, so I followed him for a while before I ran him off the cliff up at Bay Cove. But now I'm back and she is still entertaining Brick for the moment. What do you want me to do?"

When I realize what he just said, I sit up quickly and zip up my pants before I stand up and hold up my hands. Everyone stops what they are doing and stares at me.

"He is there still? Are you sure?" I ask as everyone watches me with anger in their eyes.

"Yes, so hurry before he leaves again."

"Alright, stay put. I will be right there. Give me about ten minutes." I say as everyone listens to every word that comes out of my mouth.

By the time I end the call, everyone is waving the women out and we are getting ready to go to war because the moment I kill Brick, shit is going to go down real fast. And if they haven't figured out that gear is dead, they will soon enough.

"So, while I do this, I am going to need everyone on high alert. Make sure that all the women and children are safe, and someone is with them. And I do mean everyone. You, Snake. I need you to go to Amy's place and watch over them. Keep her and Jonathan safe for me while I am gone. The rest of you, if you don't have someone to watch over, go to the edges of our territory. And do make sure that no one gets through that doesn't belong. Remember, shoot to kill if you see anyone from the other rival gang because it could mean one of ours gets killed if we don't."

After I get done barking orders, I pick up my gun and wipe it off on a towel before I place it in my waist band and head out to meet

Rider. But for some reason, the closer I get to the destination, I can't help but feel something is wrong.

## Chapter 12: Justine's Day

After breakfast, grandpa, and grandma hand me a list of necessities to get in town so I quickly grab my backpack and hurry to the car. As soon as I sit down and get buckled, I turn it on and hit the button on the radio. Instantly, rock music blares out of the speakers as I look in the rearview mirror at my reflection.

Today, I've decided to put on makeup and do my hair for once in hopes of seeing "him".

"I wonder if he is thinking about me right now?" I murmur under my breath as I wink seductively and then look behind me to make sure no one is coming.

As I put it into gear, I back up without looking the other way and nearly hit a red truck speeding past me.

"Damn, that would have been the end of me for sure. I must remember to look both ways next time before I back out." I say as I grip the wheel tightly and take a deep breath in to calm my nerves.

When I feel that I can drive safely, I continue to the town square where I park my car and then walk to my first stop. Then I look up at the old street sign that says Crescent Bay Post Office, I smile and open the door before I walk in. At first glance, it looks tiny until you walk through the entryway, and it opens into a spacious hall with a front desk and an area for all the post boxes.

The walls are painted pastel blue like the sky and the boxes all have gold trim on them.

"How may I help you?" Mr. Partridge asks while he stares at me happily.

"I have a few letters to send out. Say, have you ever been to Tennessee? I am thinking of moving there for a job offer."

"No, I can't say I have. But Marilyn used to live there when she was younger. She always talks about it and says she misses that southern drawl, and the way people tend to care more about each other." He replies softly while staring out the window behind me.

"Well, if all works out, I won't be seeing you around for a while. I do plan on coming back for vacation days to visit but that may be a year or two. After all, I haven't exactly figured out what kind of schedule I will have yet if I decide to accept."

"Oh? It sounds like you may be hesitant about leaving your family behind. Don't be. I assure you they will always be here if you change your mind. Sure, this little town has its share of problems, but for those of us who are still refusing to leave, we intend on hanging in here for quite a while." He states in a matter-of-fact tone of voice as he takes my letters and then hands me a receipt. "Will there be anything else?" he adds as he stares at me.

"No, I think I am good. Thanks though. I feel a lot better about it all and maybe I will take them up on their offer after all." I say as I begin to think of all the possibilities that moving to Tennessee would have to offer.

For one, I am sure that "he" won't be anywhere near there. Another thing is that I will have a fresh start where no one will know my family or what I have done in the past. Perhaps, this is exactly what I need to finally move past my family's dark clouds.

As I turn around, I quickly say, "Thanks again for the talk. I think I will try it on for size. After all, it can't possibly be any worse than here."

"Well, let me know how it goes." He yells after me as I open the door and walk down the street with a renewed sense of hope.

Realizing that I have just made the biggest decision of my life, I finally feel at peace with myself. I smile bigger than I have in a very long time, not since I was a small child.

It makes me feel wonderful to know that I am leaving this God forsaken place and all the bad people behind. But at the same time, I know I will miss my grandparents with all my heart and soul because they are all I have left in this world that I care about.

"Hey, I haven't seen you in a long time." Nancy says as she walks up to me, and we cross at the corner.

I continue walking while I reply quickly, "I have been mainly staying at home out of trouble."

But then I stop dead in my tracks when we reach the other side as I look over and notice a biker that looks strangely familiar. However, he is no longer wearing a suit. Now he is in a snug fitting black t-shirt and jeans. They look so good on him that I completely forget that I am supposed to be talking to Nancy.

When I look up into his eyes, I realize he is staring back at me, and I feel that electricity flow through me again like a spark that won't quit.

"Justine." Nancy says as she raises her voice, and it finally snaps me out of my trance.

"Come on."

"Oh, sorry. I was spacing out there for a minute. I most likely will be moving to Tennessee for that job because they ended up offering it to me, and I really think I will take it." I say quietly as I begin to walk faster now.

Why is it right when I start to forget about this town, "he" always shows up to make me want to stay and find out more about him? Just my fucking luck!

Nancy Monroe has been a friend since the first day of kindergarten. Mrs. Gamble sat us next to each other in the seating chart and from then on, we have been friends through thick and thin. My one and only true friend in this small town with so many secrets.

"Oh, Justine I am so proud of you. I know you have been trying to leave for a while now and I am glad it is finally working out for you. But I will miss you something terribly." She pauses and then adds with a smirk on her lips as her chestnut brown hair blows in the wind, "Unless….I come with you. Hear me out. We can get an apartment together and I can find a job doing dishes or something at one of the cafes there. I am sure they will have something for me to do."

I stop to think about it for a moment and begin to laugh before suggesting sarcastically, "You know. I can't believe I am saying this but that might work."

"Well, why don't you call me in a few days when you know more for sure, and we will start packing then. Does that sound like a plan?" she asks while staring at me with wide eyes full of excitement.

I nod, and then state, "This is me. I have to pick up a new chainsaw for grandpa and then a few groceries for grandma before heading back. I will get a hold of you as soon as I figure out when and where."

"Awesome. I just can't wait. See you later."

The moment I walk into the hardware store, I start to feel worse because several of my dad's gang are standing at the counter. "Yeah, we need a few 4 by 8 pieces of plywood and some 2 by 4's. Plus, some of those thicker nails over there." One of them says, as they point the nails out to Mr. Smith the owner.

I hesitate to approach them, but when another one walks up behind me and squeezes past me, I am forced to do something. So, I swallow hard and walk towards them with a smile. As soon as the tallest one sees me, he smirks and then says snidely, "Hey, look who's here. Too good to hang around with the likes of us? Huh?"

One of them punches him and says in a gruff and deeper voice, "Knock it the fuck off. Just leave her alone. She didn't do anything to you."

"Man, fuck you. It really sounds like to me that you are busy trying to get in her pants. I mean, if I thought I had a chance with her, I would be whispering sweet nothings into her ear before I bent her over the counter and listened to her scream my name."

"What? Help me help me?" Another one jokes before they all look at each other and start to laugh loudly.

"Actually, I would knee you in the groin and then laugh at your micro penis. My grandpa is always saying that guys that run their mouths are just compensating for their inadequacies." I yell suddenly and then they all stop to stare at me.

"Alright, here is your stuff. Why don't you guys just get out of here and leave the paying customers alone?" Mr. Smith says angrily as he gestures to the door.

For a moment they look at each other and then laugh before the tallest one takes the wood and says, "Alright, I guess the fun is over. Let's get this fixed before the storm hits this evening."

They all nod, and then I quickly skirt to the side so they can get past me without touching me.

"So, are you here for a chainsaw?" he asks and then waits for my answer.

I nod, and then he adds happily, "Your grandfather and I had a talk the other day because his chainsaw was wearing out. I thought it might be the case when I saw you stop in. But then again you never know around here."

"Yeah, he sent me to pick up a new one because nothing ever lasts forever."

"I don't know about that. Me and the misses have been together for 50 years now and if that doesn't qualify as forever, I don't know what does." He says as we walk over to the chainsaws, and he picks one up for me and puts it over on the counter.

"That will be $398.00 today." He says before I hand him 4 crisp $100 hundred dollar bills.

After he gives me the change he adds sweetly, "If you want to pull the car around to the front, I will run it out for you."

"O.K. but give me a little bit. I need to get grandma a few things from the grocery store before I grab the car. Thank you."

Once I get a few groceries, I walk back to the car quickly and put them away in the backseat before picking up the chainsaw and heading home. On the way, all I can think about is the conversation Nancy and I had and what I am going to do about it. That is until I run the stop sign by the house and out of nowhere a motorcycle slams into the side of the car making a loud metallic crashing sound.

## Chapter 13: What Happened?

From the moment I pull up next to Rider's car, I can tell that something is wrong because he is sitting in the driver's seat completely still. If he were watching Tonya's house, he would not be in his car clear down the road. So, I cautiously walk up to his window and look in.

"Damn it." I murmur under my breath.

I was right. From behind you can't see the bright red blood gushing from the bullet hole in his temple or the way his eyes look with that blank expression on them. How did they get to such an expert killer? Surely, he would have caught movement around him and been able to shoot them before they did him in.

Now as I gaze at Tonya's house, I can tell that they are all long gone. The house is dark, and all the vehicles have disappeared without a trace. I just can't believe that they took out Rider and put him in his car between the time he called, and I arrived.

All this, and I spared no time getting here. Yet somehow, they managed to be one step ahead again. Do I have another mole in the club house? If so, who then?

Think Angel. Think. How would they have known that Rider was there? And more importantly how did they get a leg up on a hired hitman?

Just then a thought crossed my mind. When the phone call came in, Sara and Monica were in the room. They heard everything. Could it have been one of them? They would have had enough time to call Brick after they left and before I could get here.

"Those stupid cunts!" I growl as the thoughts begin to spin around my head.

I immediately pick up my phone and dial Tiny. When he doesn't pick up right away, I get ready to call Trouble but then I hear Tiny's voice answer, "What's up? Did you get him?"

"No, change of plans. Rider is dead."

"What?" Tiny yells over the phone as it echoes through my head.

"Sorry, I didn't mean to yell but what the fuck just happened? Are you O.K.?" he asks softly now as I hear a woman's voice in the background and realize that it is Monica.

"Don't say anymore. I think one of the girls is in on it and it could possibly be Monica."

"Sure thing, boss." He replies quickly before I hear him raise his voice and add loudly, "Bitch, get out of here. I need to go."

She starts to yell something before Tiny announces, 'You are going to get out of here now before I throw your stinky ass out."

I hear a door slam and then Tiny states, "She is finally gone. So, you really think it is her?"

"Possibly. The alternative is that it is either Sara or one of the guys is working with them. But I would rather not think about that right now because then I won't know who I can trust anymore."

"True. This really sucks. So, what can I do Boss?" he asks quietly before waiting for my answer.

"Just sit tight. I will call you when I know more."

When I hang up, I go back to Rider's car and then fish out his phone from his jacket pocket. The last thing I need right now is for the cops to find my phone number in his call log as the last number he dialed before he was shot. Then I sit there for a few minutes to figure out what is next.

After I decide what to do, I drive to clear my head. Drive out into the country where the sky is bluer than it is anywhere else. However, when I take my eyes off the road for a moment and slow down, I slam into a car.

A sharp pain spreads through my head as I hit the ground and I thank God that I remembered to wear my helmet. Everything turns in circles as I watch a familiar woman walk up to me and kneel by my side.

"I am so sorry. I don't know how this happened. Are you alright?" she asks sadly while I peel off my mask and then pull off my helmet only to see a big crack in it.

"It's not that bad. You certainly don't have to cry for me. I assure you I will be fine because I have been hit much harder than this before and walked away from it."

Just as soon as the world stops spinning, I sit up and then ask her frankly, "By the way, where the fuck did you come from?"

She hesitates and furrows her beautiful brow before she finally answers with a sad little frown, "I'm sorry. I wasn't paying attention so I must have run the stop sign."

"It could have been worse, but damn that hurt. I don't suppose you would kiss my booboos, would you?" I ask sarcastically as I wipe the gravel off my clothes and find myself gazing back into her amazing eyes.

Shocked, she just stares at me, and I can only guess that she pretends not to hear that last part because then she stands up and offers a hand. "I am Justine. I have seen you around town here and I was curious about something. I saw you at the funeral and I wondered if you were from here. Or are you just visiting?"

Before I say a word, I take her warm hand and stand up as I answer her, but I refuse to let go, "First of all, everyone around here calls me Angel, and yes, I am from here, but I left for a while. I suppose I tried to leave this life behind me and escape but one never truly does. Of course, you of all people should know that. I was told that you are

Brick's daughter. By the way, I am your father's enemy, and we probably should not be talking to each other, but for some reason I can't stop."

When she doesn't fight my touch, I realize that she seems to feel the same way. So, I lean down and tangle my fingers in her silky hair before kissing her soft lips hard. Our eyes lock on each other as a deep moan escapes my throat and then I hear a squeak so soft that I can barely hear it leave her lips.

It's admittedly cute, so cute that I just want to eat her up right here and now, but I stop and release her as I search her eyes for answers.

"Why did you stop? Not good enough for you?" she says sarcastically as the hurt in her voice tells me what I need to know.

After I lift her up effortlessly with one arm and she wraps her slender legs around my waist, I carry her over to the car while devouring her sweet mouth. When I search her eyes again and see what I am looking for, I sit her on the hood before my fingers trail up to the soft skin of her neck and close around it. As I tighten my grip, I shove her down on her back violently and the metal makes a loud banging sound.

Right away, I notice that she relaxes into it as if she has done this countless times before. Yet, I choose to ignore it when I decide to fuck her right here and now. So, I instantly stop kissing her to release my tight grip on her neck and reach for my pants. When I feel the cool metal of the zipper, I look at my handprint on her flesh and stop to smile. However, just as need surges through me like a racehorse, I hear the sirens blare behind me as Tony hits them to alert us to his approach.

I turn around quickly and swear under my breath, "Son of a bitch."

With a shit eating grin, he gets out of his police cruiser while holding his hands in the air.

"Hey, buddy. I heard there was a possible accident. Am I right? Is everyone O.K.? Or do I need to call for an ambulance?"

"If you don't get out of here, you will need an ambulance, Tony." I say in a deep growl as I look between the two of them.

"Actually, I need to have a little talk with you over here. Right now." He says as he gestures for me to walk over to his car.

When we are out of Justine's ear shot, Tony says quietly, "You do know that she is Brick's daughter right? If he catches you fucking her, there will be all out war and I can't have that on my streets. Got it."

I pause before answering reluctantly, "He already started it, but understood. You don't realize just how lucky you are to be my friend. If any other cop would have told me what to do, I may have been forced to lay down my law."

"Well, I am your friend so let it go for now. Please. Trust me some things are just not worth it." He says as he stares at me and then glances over to where Justine is now leaning against the car.

"I will take care of this. As long as your bike is still working, I won't call this in, but you had better get out of here."

For the moment he is right, so I look at Justine one last time before I walk over to my hog, and I pick it up. When I get on and start the engine, I slip my helmet and mask back on before I leave. But as I drive off, I can still hear Tony yelling, "Don't forget tonight." In the distance.

## Chapter 14: Revenge Is A Two Edged Sword

After leaving the scene of the accident, I drive back to Amy's house to make sure everything is alright there.

"Amy, did Snake ever show up?" I yell anxiously when I find that the front door is unlocked, and Snake's bike isn't in the driveway.

At first, I don't hear an answer, so I go from room to room methodically until I find her asleep in Jonathan's bedroom. When I see her sitting in the rocker snoring like a chainsaw, I breathe a sigh of relief before I quietly shut the door behind me and walk out to the living room. "Where is he?" I murmur under my breath as I pull out my phone and call him.

It rings several times and then instantly goes to voice mail, so I hang up and call again. When he doesn't pick up the second time, I decide that I need to wake Amy up. After opening the door quietly, I creep over to Jonathan first and gaze down at the most incredibly cute sleeping monster. Then I smile before turning my attention to his mother.

She is sleeping so comfortably that I don't want to wake her, but I need to know where Snake is and why he left so I gently shake her arm before saying, "Amy, wake up."

Her eyes open a bit and then when she sees me staring at her, they open completely before she sits up and asks sleepily, "Is Jonathan O.K.?"

"Yes. But Amy, did Snake ever come by today?" I ask carefully without saying too much because I don't want to alarm her.

She shakes her head no, and then her eyes start to close again before I ask, "Are you sure he hasn't come by?"

"I am positive. No one has been here but you. Why?" she asks now with concern in her eyes.

"Because I specifically told him to come here and stay put. He was to watch over you and Jonathan because Brick's right-hand man is dead. But now it is so much worse than that. Rider is dead too."

"What…..How?" she asks quickly as she looks over at Jonathan with a furrowed brow.

"They shot him while he was watching Tonya's house, and I am afraid we have another traitor in the midst. That is why I was so concerned when I arrived, and Snake was not here protecting the two of you."

"Do you think he is involved?" she asks hesitantly as she picks up Jonathan to feed him.

I mull this thought around in my head until I finally speak again a few minutes later, "I don't know. Maybe it is best that we don't talk about this right now until I figure out where exactly he is because someone must pay for Rider's death as well as Sledge's."

"What? Sledge is dead?"

"Yes, they took him out while we were waiting at the club house. He was on his way, and they jumped him at Dead Man's Curve." I say sadly as I close my eyes and wish that I had my hands around Brick's neck right now.

Jonathan starts crying on cue, so she sits down in the rocking chair and pulls her shirt open for him to feed. I take that as my excuse to leave so I exit the room and take my phone out to call Hawk.

"We have a problem. Snake is MIA and Rider is dead. I don't know if Snake has switched sides or is caught up in all of this. For all I know he could be dead in the ditch somewhere too. We need to all meet back up at the club house pronto to figure out what to do." I say quietly so Amy doesn't hear the conversation.

As I walk out the front door, I lock it behind me. But before I leave, I end the call and then proceed to look around cautiously scanning the neighboring houses for anything suspicious. When I see nothing, I head back to meet up with everyone else.

On my way, I drive by Milly's quickly and spot Brick walking in with Tonya.

"Stupid fucking cunt!" I murmur under my breath as I turn the corner and then speed to the club house.

When I arrive, I see Austin leaning against his bike and Tiny standing next to him discussing something. They quickly look up at me and then nod, before Tiny says loudly, "Hey boss, so Hawk filled us in. Now what?"

"Well, let's talk about this inside. The last thing we need right now is for anyone else to hear this." I say authoritatively as I walk in.

The moment the doors slam shut I look around to see Buzz sitting at the bar. Trouble is standing a few feet away talking with Sara and Hawk is sitting in the chair next to mine by the head of the table. A few of the other boys that I don't really know yet, sit down when they see me arrive. Instantly, I feel on edge because Sara begins to stare at me, and Monica is nowhere to be found. Either one of them could be in on it so I need to get rid of her before we continue our talk.

"Do you mind?" I ask as I point at the exit while staring right back at her.

When she doesn't get it right away, I yell, "Get the fuck out. It is time for business not pleasure."


As soon as she hears me say those words, she walks quickly to the door and slams it upon her exit.

"Good riddance." I murmur as I stare at everyone left in the room.

"So, does anyone know where Snake is now? Or have any of you seen him since he left here?" I ask as Tiny and Austin walk in behind me and take a seat at the table.

They all look casually at each other and then shake their heads slowly.

"So, no one has seen him? Is that right? Don't you think that a bit odd?" I ask before licking my lower lip slowly and thinking about the fact that he disappeared right after we all left here.

"Where could he have gone? I just drove by Milly's, and I didn't see his bike there with them."

Right as I am about to sit down, my phone rings. An unknown number pops up on my screen as I pull it out quickly from my jeans. I hesitate, but then I get a funny feeling, so I decide to hit the answer button and put it on speaker.

"You have until 9 tonight to pack up your bags and get your gang out of town. Or you will find pieces of your buddy here strewn all over the Bay tomorrow." A deep voice states snidely over the phone.

"Don't do it. You know what you have to do." Snake yells and then I hear a blood curdling scream a second before the phone call ends.

When I realize that the phone call has ended, I glance quickly at all the shocked faces. Every one of them knows full well what we must do now. If we want to help Snake and stay in Crescent Bay, we must kill them all now.

As I sit there contemplating our next move, I look down at my watch to see that it is already 1 p.m. and that means we only have 8 hours supposedly before they kill him. However, we all know that they will torture him long before then so whatever we are going to do, we need to start on right away.

"Alright, listen up. Austin, get all the guns out of the locker because I want everyone to have a shotgun, plenty of ammo and their personal weapons on them at all times. We are going to Milly's at 4 p.m. and kill every single one of them. There is no other option."

"O.K., but shouldn't someone get all the women and children together and bring them here so a few of us can watch over them in one place? Wouldn't it be safer?" Tiny asks as he stands up and walks over to where I am standing.

"Yes, you have a good point. I will head over to Amy's right now and make sure they get here safely. As for the rest of you, get your families here quickly. We need to get this all buttoned up before it gets completely out of control." I bark as I walk towards the door.

## Chapter 15: Justine's Luck

"I can't believe my luck." I murmur under my breath as the cop finally pulls away and leaves me to sit there all alone for a moment.

What is wrong with me? I just can't believe that I was about to let him screw me in public like that. I mean what the hell was I thinking? I wasn't and that is the problem. He is my family's enemy, and they kill each other for a living. The worst part is that if this shit keeps up, I am going to get caught in the middle and end up dead too.

"Man, I just need to get out of this town before something really bad happens."

As I slam my forehead into the steering wheel an image crosses my mind of him pressing his full weight against me, filling me completely. Instantly, my body begins to react when I think of how his hard balls would feel smacking against my sensitive clit as he bends me over the hood. What would that have felt like if we hadn't been rudely interrupted? The word "Incredible" erupts from my throat quietly as a secretive smile slowly spreads across my lips.

"Now I know what heaven feels like." I say breathlessly when I start to relive our brief encounter over and over in my mind.

The electricity in every touch, and the way his body fit mine. We are perfect for each other in every single way but one. Oh, how I ache for him even though he could never be mine.

While I sit there for a few more minutes, I make up my mind to get him out of my head and move on.

"As soon as I get home, I really need to call them to accept the job before they offer it to someone else." I remind myself as I focus on the road and start the car.

The moment I turn the radio back on, a song plays that reminds me of my mom. So, I begin to remember all the things we used to do together in the summers before she died. One of her favorite places was the beach down at Fernandos. We would play for hours making sandcastles and then we would swim even if we didn't have swimming suits.

Everyone would stare at us, but we didn't care because we had each other and that was enough.

"I wish I could turn back time." I murmur softly as I wipe the tears out of my eyes.

I clear my throat and then add in a whisper, "But I need to stop this shit because I am an adult and adults move on. After all, I have a new life to live, and Nancy is going to come with me, so I really need to just suck it up and grow a pair."

Realizing that I have been sitting here for far too long, I look in my review mirror before pulling back out onto the road. For the moment, there is no one coming so I begin to speed and turn up the radio so loud that the door starts to vibrate. Then I sing along with the new, much happier song as I break 80 on the speedometer and smile from ear to ear because I know something that only a few others do. By tomorrow morning, I will be getting out of here.

Unfortunately, my happy thoughts are cut short when I see a motorcycle turn the corner and speed towards me. It looks familiar and as soon as it passes me, I already know too late that it is my father.

"Shit." I swear loudly as I watch him turn around quickly in my rearview mirror.

When he catches up to me in no time flat, he flags me over to the side of the road, so I hesitantly slow down to a stop as I pull off. I instinctively shrink down in my seat and groan while he gets off his bike and walks up to my window with that scummy look on his face.

"Justine. Roll it down. It's really important that I talk to you." He says with a furrowed brow as he gestures for me to lower it.

I frown and then do it reluctantly while turning down the radio before he starts to demand, "You need to come with me. Gear is dead and I am afraid you may be on their list too to get to me. The only way I will feel better about all of this is if you are with me at Milly's because then I can personally keep an eye on you."

As soon as I hear him say it, I swallow hard and shake my head. There is no way in hell I am going anywhere with him. Especially, to their gang hang out. That is the last thing I will ever do if I can help it.

"Damn it Justine. Now is not the time to defy me. This is a life-or-death situation and I need to be able to count on the fact that you will listen to me for once in your life.

You're my daughter. Now start acting like it!" he yells as his face contorts angrily and he slams his fists into the top of the car.

I shrink back down in hopes that he doesn't decide to take his anger out on me. I know that when I was younger mom would often come home with black eyes and bruises on her body. She always told grandma and grandpa that there was a motorcycle accident, but we all knew better. Then when she died, we knew that he was to blame.

"I refuse to live in your shadow anymore. I am leaving tomorrow for good and there is nothing you can do about it." I yell right back at him when I finally summon enough courage to tell him off before I add hatefully, "Besides, I would rather stand my ground with grandma and grandpa then you any day."

"Why you little bitch!" he replies loudly as he starts to raise his hand to back hand me.

I promptly shut the window and put my foot on the gas as I drive away. When I glance behind me in the mirror, all I see is him screaming something angrily as dust swirls around him.

"Finally." I murmur as I breathe a huge sigh of relief and then continue down the road.

As I pass my turn to go home, I keep driving because I need to do some thinking without anyone interrupting me. A few miles later, I see the bay to the left side of me and decide to go take a quick dip to clear my head.

"There we go." I say softly as I stop and look out the front window at the shimmering water in front of me.

Once I am out of the car and leaning up against the closed door, I slip my shoes off and close my eyes before feeling the warm breeze on my skin. Then I walk down to the water's edge as it creeps over my toes and splashes on my rolled-up pant legs. It feels so deliciously wonderful that I find myself never wanting to leave it. So, I sit down right then and there on the wet sand and soak up the rays for what seems like hours.

## Chapter 16: Is It Meant To Be?

While thinking about what must be done, I drive by the beach on the way to Amy's to calm down. Of course, as I glance over at the water quickly, I catch a glimpse of "her" relaxing in the sand as if her whole world isn't about to just come crumbling down around her. Is she absolutely oblivious to everything that has been going on? Or does she simply not care at all?

Either way, I refuse to think about her soft skin against mine and the way her neck fit perfectly in my hand. Or the fact that every time I turn around, she is there taunting me. How does she even do that?

As a matter of fact, I hate her for the way she makes me feel when I think about her and how she invades my every waking moment.

"This just has to fucking stop!" I yell at myself as I glance back over at her lying there so peacefully.

Do I keep riding past? Or stop and get this whole thing over with once and for all so I can take care of business. If I have to fuck her so I can concentrate, so be it.

After deciding what must be done, I slam on the brakes and quickly turn around before I change my mind. It was so easy before I came back here, but now nothing is simple. When I pull up next to her car, I kick the stand down and take off my mask before climbing off the bike.

"I really shouldn't be here right now." I warn as I hang my mask and helmet on the handlebar before taking my boots off and leaving them next to the bike.

"It's only a matter of time before someone sees us together and the shit starts to fly." I say as I shake my head in disgust and walk towards where she is laying.

She must hear me coming, because a few minutes later she opens her eyes and sits up as she stares at me with those hauntingly beautiful eyes.

"I need to have a talk with you." I say as I watch her stand up and glare at me.

"I have had quite enough of everyone having to talk to me today. First my dad and now you. I am not a child who needs scolding, I am a grown ass woman." She shouts at me while continuing to glare.

This is not the woman I met just an hour or so before. What on earth happened to her? Realizing that she was talking about Brick, I say quickly just in case he is still hanging around, "Come with me under the dock. I don't think we should be seen together right now."

"And what makes you think that? Did you kill Gear like he said you did?" she replies as I grab her hand tightly and begin to pull her towards the rocks.

When she fights me, I get angry and growl, "You will listen to me. Now."

I guess I take her by surprise because she gives up the fight right away and lets me lead her to the shaded area by the cement pillars out of the way of prying eyes. Then I release her hand temporarily while I scan the area to make sure that no one saw where we went.

"You are just like my dad." She says accusingly with hatred in her voice.

Before she can say anymore, I slam her up against the cement and devour her lips just to shut her up. But then I taste her, and I can't stop myself from exploring every crevice of her mouth. My fingers find her silky raven hair and tighten around it before I yank her head back so I can look deeper into her eyes.

As I continue to kiss her and bite her lips, she kisses me back as she presses her stomach against my shaft. He instinctively jerks to the left when I feel her hand slink between us, and her petite fingers latch on to him through the cloth of my pants. However, when I can't take it anymore, my hand raises to her neck quickly so I can hold her in place to unzip my pants. But instead of freeing him right away, she places her other hand on top of mine while she begs me to, "Please, keep squeezing" and stares at me with wide eyes.

I stop to think about this for merely a second and then say softly with a smirk, "Your wish is my command." before I continue to tighten my fingers around her soft skin.

As I look down into her eyes, I release him from my pants, and she automatically starts to stroke him with a tight fist. Just how I like it. Amazing.

Slowly, she continues to the tip as she pulls it towards her, and we alternate kissing and biting each other hungrily. But when she begins to tighten her grip, my breathing becomes labored, and I moan deeply. At the same time, I still manage to notice that she is becoming unsteady, so I release my hand from around her neck.

After I do, she glances up at me with those big puppy dog eyes again as I shove her back against the cement. Within a second or two, I have her pants unbuttoned before I forcefully pull them down to her knees in one movement and see that she is shaved. Then I scoop her up in my arms and carry her over to the platform as quickly as I can.

I need to be in her so bad that it feels as if my life depends on it.

"Are you clean?" I ask as she looks back at me with bruised lips from our kisses and a red handprint around her neck.

She nods quickly and then grasps for my clothes as she pulls at my pants. Apparently, she needs me as much as I do her. When I see this, I decide to help her out by pulling my jeans down and watching as he springs to attention.

"I need him in me now, please." She mews as she scoots up higher on the platform to lay down and spreads her legs for me after she pulls her pants off and throws them on the sand.

As I place my hands on the rough cement, I feel a cool breeze from the water blowing against my skin. I take the time to close my eyes for a second and sigh before I slide my palms up her thighs to her hips and dig my fingers in. However, the second my head brushes against her slit, I feel it. This unexplainable electricity that flows between us and when I slowly slide into her, I feel like I am alive for the first time in my life.

Everything is right for once when I lean down to lick her nipple and then thrust deep inside. She cries out as she grasps the stubble on top of my head, and she clamps down on my rock-hard cock. At that moment, I couldn't be happier because for some reason I feel like this is meant to be.

Even if I am supposed to be someplace else because people are counting on me.

When she begins to lick my earlobe and then bites down hard, I slide out and then thrust in even harder to punish her for it.

"Fuck. This feels so incredible, like you were made for me. Baby, you are perfect in every way." I say as I stare into her eyes and see something indescribable.

"I can't right now. I need to get this out of my system by fucking the life out of her and then ending Brick before he kills all my people." I think to myself as I try to get my head in the game and finish what I started.

"Harder." She cries out as she sits up and holds onto my shoulders with her black fingernails.

Somewhere between the sounds of the water behind me and skin on skin contact, I lose my thought and start to pound her harder and harder. As I come closer to release, I slow down until she looks me straight in the eyes and yells, "I'm going to come."

Realizing that I too am about to explode, I thrust in one more time and then quickly pull out as she begins to squirt on me.

Now, I love watching a good girl squirt as much as the rest. But when she does it, it is so much hotter than with anyone else because she looks as if she is embarrassed of her own body. It makes me want to keep fucking her forever and show her that she doesn't need to be ashamed. So, I run my fingers through it slowly and then rub her clit softly with my thumb.

It seems to stop instantly, so I lean between her legs and begin to lick her clean with the flat of my tongue. She cries out and grabs my head while trying to pull me up. But I don't let her and suck her nub gently before I travel down to her soaked folds.

"God, you are so beautiful. Every single inch of you." I say as I stop and look up before tickling her entrance with my index finger.

When she seems to like it, I add softly, "That's a good girl" before I bury my face in her sweet pussy again and I feel her nails tear at my skin on my biceps.

A second later I slip it inside. She moans again and then I slide it in further slowly before she cries out, "More."

"More?"

"I will give you more. Turn over so I can fuck that ass of yours." I say impatiently because by now my balls ache so bad that I can't possibly tolerate it anymore.

Being the good girl she is, she obeys and turns over for me. As she bends over the platform, I spread her cheeks. Then I rub my tip on her rim around in a circle to tickle it before I thrust it in hard and fast.

At this point, I need to come so bad that I no longer care about anything except for my need to explode in her tight little ass.

She whimpers but then slams her ass into me and begs softly, "Harder."

Hearing those words, I raise my hand and slap her ass so hard that it leaves a handprint and the sound echoes. I smirk at my handiwork as my fingers dig into her hips and I thrust harder in. When I slide back out, I hold my breath so I can last a little longer, but it doesn't work as I shoot the cum all over her ass and make a big mess.

Afterwards, I decide to run my fingers over it and rub it into her skin because I love marking a woman like any other guy with my seed. But this one is special for some reason. So, as I slide my hand across her soft bottom and smear it all over her, a smirk plays on my lips because I own her now. She is mine.

## Chapter 17: The Dilemma

"Are you having fun?" I ask sarcastically as he continues to run his fingers across my skin.

"Yes, but I really need to go." He says softly and then pauses for a few minutes before adding hesitantly, "I probably shouldn't tell you this. But then again you may already know that your father is holding one of my men. If we don't leave town by tonight, he will kill him." He says quietly while looking around to make sure that no one hears us talking, even though that should be the least of his worries.

"My father only told me that your men killed his. He never mentioned anything else when he said that I needed to go to Milly's." I reply quickly before I realize that I should have never said it and hurry to put my fingers to my lips.

Too late because he has heard me and now stares at me as if he suddenly knows a special secret.

"Please. I may hate my father but don't hurt him because he is still my dad. Please." I beg sadly as I realize that I care for him even though he is a bad man.

He pauses for a moment while he stares at me as if he is contemplating something important. Then he leans down to kiss me softly on the lips and says in a whisper so close to my ear that I can feel his breath, "I can't promise anything because he killed my brother Drift and one of my good friends. Now, he promises to kill another. I can't let that happen no matter what has happened between the two of us."

I search his eyes for something to hold onto, but I know that he is going to leave and perhaps I will never see him again. Whether he kill my father or be killed, my world will never be the same again after tonight. When

I reach up and touch his cheek with my palm, I feel the coarse stubble brush against it as I ask quietly, "Is there any chance at all that your gang would just leave town like he wants?"

He hesitates before closing his eyes and leaning into my hand. For a few seconds there is a silence between us as I begin to understand.

I clear my throat and then begin to speak, "Revenge is bittersweet. On one hand you avenge your loved ones, but on the other it never truly solves anything. That person is dead and there is nothing you can do that will ever bring them back again. Not even killing those who harmed them. Is it worth losing your soul to bring your brother's killer to your idea of justice? I had thought that way at one time when my mother was killed four years ago. However, I soon realized that hatred only eats you up and once you allow it to consume you, you can never return to what you once were." I pause and sigh before continuing cautiously, "I know that we have only known each other a short time but I can tell that deep down you have a good soul. Please don't do this. Go. Take your people and leave before it is too late. My father has so many men. How can you possibly hope to take them all on?"

The moment I finish, he starts to shake his head while he stares at the sand below our feet. "You have no idea, do you? It is not that simple. Some of my men have families that live here. Women with children who were born in this town. I can't just upend them all and leave in one night. I can't expect that of them it's not right. This all has to stop now. We were here first, and we will be here afterwards, but The Devils Legion will be long gone if I have anything to do with it."

With that said, he promptly steps back and pulls up his pants. After zipping his jeans, he grabs mine off the sand and shakes them out before handing them to me. As he watches me get dressed, he says not a word but his eyes relay everything I need to know. He is going to kill Brick and there isn't anything I can do about it. However, on the slight chance that he decides not to, I ask quickly, "I don't suppose I will ever see you again, will I?"

He looks down briefly before gazing into my eyes and replying sadly, "I wouldn't get your hopes up. Even if we get rid of Brick's guys, I will have my hands full."

When he wipes the sand off his pants, he walks away without saying another word and never looks back at me. Because of this, I already know that I was just a moment in time and that it meant nothing in the grand scheme of things. After all, I was probably just another notch to add to his belt.

I watch as he speeds off on his bike and then I drive home. My grandparents don't say a word to me when I arrive later than usual, but I soon realize why after Brick's man

Eagle comes for me. Apparently, while I was gone, he had a talk with them, and they all agreed that Milly's would be the safest place for me. Of course, I would not find out until an hour later when Eagle mentions that Brick forcefully insisted on it.

"How dare he. Why does everyone treat me like a child?" I yell angrily as I head towards the door of the diner. "I am leaving."

"You will not." Brick barks as he grabs my forearm and yanks me towards his chest. "Justine. You are here for your own good. Whether you like it or not, this is the safest place for you right now. The other gang will do whatever they can to gain an advantage including hurting you."

I glare up at him hatefully as I claw his hands with my fingernails. When I finally make him release me, I move back quickly and head towards the exit. But as I step to the door, I hear a loud gunshot.

It shatters the window next to my head and glass sprays all over the floor. I crouch down in fear of my life and begin to shake uncontrollably. Right away, Brick grabs my hand and pulls me into the next room before shutting the door behind him.

He looks me over closely while asking, "Are you alright?"

I shake my head and reply in a scared little voice, "I think so."

"Well, I need to get back out there and figure out what is going on, but I need you to stay here. For fuck's sake please listen to me for once. I do know what I am talking about."

I lash out and grab his forearm as he turns to leave me all alone, then I ask quietly, "Do you have one of their men, father?"

He starts to laugh and then quickly turns serious as he glares at me and says mockingly, "Why do you care? You have never cared about anything I did before this? Why now?"

"Because if you do, you need to let him go. If you give a damn about me at all, you will let him leave without being harmed. Why can't everyone live here? It is big enough for all of us."

"Justine, you will never understand." He yells before I hear a barrage of gunshots fill the air with loud booming sounds and the screams from the next room become unbearable.

## Chapter 18: It's Now Or Never

It's just shortly after 8 p.m. when I walk into the bar and see Tony sitting there with his hat laying on the counter. He is still wearing his uniform, but he has it unbuttoned so I can see the large heart tattoo just below the neckline of his white undershirt. When he notices me standing there, he glances over at me and waves with a big smile on his face.

"Hey, over here." He says a bit too loudly as he draws attention from everyone.

I nod, and smile in return as I quickly walk over to him and sit down.

"I only have a few minutes, but I really could use your help. I know that we have not always seen eye to eye and occasionally we have been on the opposite sides of the law." I say as I start to laugh before furrowing my brow.

"But we don't have nearly enough men for what I am about to propose, and I could really use your gun at my side. Of course, this would have to be strictly off the clock because what we are about to do is not exactly law abiding. Understood?" I continue quietly as a tall man in a suit looks far too long at us and I end up glaring at him, so he finally stops.

"Yeah, I do. So, do I have time to grab my street clothes from the car and change?" he asks hesitantly as he looks around the bar one last time and stops on the 20 some year-old waitress with red hair and freckles.

I nod, and then he quickly walks out to his car and grabs them before disappearing into the bathroom. When he returns, he looks nothing like the cop that went in just a few moments before. Instead, he looks much more comfortable now and ready for war.

"Let's head on out." I say as I leave a 20-dollar bill on the counter to pay for his drink and stand up.

I survey the room one more time before we walk out the door. As I breathe in the warm air, he gets in his old beat-up Chevy pickup and waits for me to take the lead. Then I climb on my bike before slipping on my mask and helmet. When I am ready, I rev the engine and feel the power as I realize that this may very well be the last time, I ever ride it. God, I hope not but then again one never knows when your time has ended on this earth.

After pulling out of the driveway, we head to Milly's, for the fight of our lives.

"Now, head towards the back. When I whistle break it down!" I exclaim as I point to the rear of the diner.

Buzz and Crow nod in understanding as I watch them cautiously walk towards the alley and then head towards the backdoor. Now, it's time to get Snake back before we level the place to the ground. When I whistle, I hear a loud crash and then screaming as we continue to spray the front of the building with bullets to keep them inside so they can't leave with him. However, what I hear next I am not completely prepared for.

"Angel, please stop." Justine cries out as the door opens slowly and she emerges in front of Brick who is now wearing a sick smirk on his lips as if he knows something I don't.

"I had her followed earlier to make sure she wasn't hurt and to my surprise I found that you were fucking my daughter. How long has this been going on?" he asks snidely while looking between the two of us.

As I stand there in shock, I feel Tony jab me in the side and that is just enough to snap me out of it so I can think. When I realize what must happen, I quickly turn around and whisper to Hawk, "You know what to do. Take your shot just as soon as you can but don't take it until she is clear. Understood?"

"Yes, fully." He replies with a cold hard stare before he steps back and gets in position with his rifle.

When it is trained on Brick, he waits for his opening.

"Please let me go. I have nothing to do with your war, father. I hate everything that it stands for because it ultimately killed my mother. Don't you see that it will just be the end of all of us if you keep going?" she asks sadly as he wraps his arms around her neck and holds her tightly against him to block our bullets like a coward.

"Take the shot." I mouth to Hawk when I see an opening as Brick briefly turns to the side and stares at one of his people.

The shot rings out into the night air as he releases Justine, and she falls to the ground. Immediately, I think the worst and almost run to her. However, when Brick begins to faulter and bright red blood flows from a gaping hole in his chest, I realize that the bullet found its true owner.

He stares at me for a few seconds longer before he falls to the ground in a clump and Justine begins to sob uncontrollably. All his men step back and rush inside the diner to regroup as Justine sits on the ground with her father in her arms. She continues to cry softly as I rush to her side and collect her before any of his men decide to come out and take a shot at us.

When I see Trouble go around to the back, I realize that Buzz and Crow have not been seen since they went to retrieve Snake. So, I quickly drag Justine to the safety of Tony's truck and then attend to business.

A moment later, I am at the rear as I listen for movement inside and wait for the opportunity to present itself. Then when I hear Trouble yell, "Get the back door." I open it and prepare for the worst. But when Buzz, Crow, and Trouble carry Snake out in their arms, I breathe a sigh of relief.

Right away I help them before I see one of Brick's men come running and yelling, "They are getting away." So, I aim and take my shot before I shoot him in the head and blood sprays everywhere.

Not only did we get Snake back, but we took care of Brick. Even though I didn't get to do it myself, I still feel that we have avenged Sledge and my brother.

"He is bleeding out!" Tony yells as he points at Tiny who is laying on the dirt with a puddle of dark red blood pooling around him.

On closer inspection, I note that there is a bullet hole in his abdomen. From experience I know that he won't last for more than a few minutes, so I rush over to him and put my hand under his head. I say softly, "You did great, and we got Snake back. Just hold on. I will have Tony call an ambulance."

Before I ever manage to get that last part out, his head goes limp and his eyes stare at me blankly. He was a good man, better than most of us. But someday we will all go this way if we don't change our ways.

When I look up at Hawk, I demand before I stand up and ready my weapon, "Get them out of town now! We are done here."

"I am going to ram the front door with the car. Just make sure to cover me." Austin yells as he runs to it and gets in.

A barrage of bullets sprays the windows as he prepares to ram it at full force.

"Get over there and cover him from the side and you go to the back so we can make sure they know we mean business." I yell as a few of the gang rush around in different directions.

Even though I had temporarily forgotten about Justine, she pops in my head, and I immediately want to rush to her side, but I know that I have other priorities.

"First things first." I murmur under my breath as I watch my men work.

From inside the building, there is a loud bang before Austin rams the front and the door caves in. As soon as he backs up, they all come running out and I yell, "Leave town now and we won't kill you all. Do not come back or you won't see tomorrow. This is our town."

While I wait there with my gun in hand, ready to shoot, if necessary, I watch the last of them leave. Eventually, my men come out the front and give all clear. I in turn, walk over to them and pat them on the back for a good day's work. After all, I could have never did it without every single one of them.

"Where is Tony?" Hawk asks as he looks around the group and doesn't see him.

Immediately, I begin to scan the group and then see him lying by the truck. I rush over to him and find that he has been shot in the leg and it is slowly bleeding. When Justine sees me approach, she climbs out and starts to cry softly and tears cascade down her cheeks, "This is all my fault. When he heard my panicked screaming, he came over to make sure that I was alright. But just as soon as he turned around, a bullet hit him. I didn't know what to do because the bullets kept coming so I hid."

Shaking my head, I crouch down and tell Tony, "I will call an ambulance right away. Just don't move."

"That's the bitch. Right there." Austin yells angrily as he points at Justine.

I swing around and immediately go to her defense as I grab her and hold her behind me tightly.

"She is not a bitch, and you will not touch her over my dead body. Get that?" I declare as I growl and stare at him menacingly.

And just like that, I turn against the men that I just fought so closely with over a woman of all things.

"She is mine and no one will touch her." I bark as I stare at each of them in warning.

"Angel, you have lost it" Trouble states as he stares between us and then adds, "Once you told me to never let a woman get between us. Well, you have. So, what gives?"

"She can't help who her father was, and she never had anything to do with this war. She is innocent." I yell before I grit my teeth and add, "But if she wasn't, I would be the first to get rid of her. You know it."

"So, you are just going to let it go?" Buzz asks Trouble before he pulls his pistol and holds it to Justine from the side.

I turn to try and block him but, in that time, I hear him cock it and raise to aim. Instantly, I whip my gun around and shoot him in the chest. It takes him a second for it to register that I just shot him, but when it does, he furrows his brow in shock and falls to the ground as the blood begins to stain his white t-shirt.

Before any more of them try it, I raise my hands and yell, "She is innocent. I had to do it."

Trouble shakes his head again and then steps in front of me so no one else will try. "I get it now. She is to you, like Amy was to Drift. Brother, she can either be your greatest strength or your Kryptonite. Just be careful of which. You decide."

After he says it, everyone seems to calm down. A few of them take care of Buzz's body as I call an ambulance for Tony and look after him until it gets there.

## Chapter 19: Justine's Heart

We were sitting in the middle of the hospital while waiting to find out about Tony when this overwhelming feeling of emptiness hit me harder than a ton of bricks.
Immediately, I close my eyes so Angel can't see the tears that are threatening to escape.

"I am going to the café. Do you want a coffee or something?" Angel asks sweetly as he looks at me with concern on his handsome face.

I look up at him as a stray tear falls and at that moment, I wish I could just reach over and help him to understand how I feel. But the problem is that I don't even know why I feel this way. Let alone how to explain it.

All I know is that when my dad was killed, I felt like a piece of me was buried with him, even though I hated him with all my being.

How could I give a shit that he is gone when he ended up killing my mother in one way or another? This is stupid Justine. Just stupid. Get over it.

"Yes, I could really use a cup of coffee. Maybe it will help with my headache." I say so it masks why I really feel so damn bad.

"Oh, I could get a nurse so they can get you something for it." He replies softly as he looks around us and then stands up quickly before rushing after a nurse.

I guess it is good that he doesn't know my true thoughts because he would probably tell me I am stupid too for crying over a man who used his own daughter as a shield. After all, I doubt Angel would ever do that to anyone. He seems like he would go to hell and back for me if he needed to. As a matter of fact, I know he would.

As I find myself thinking about this, I realize that I have stopped crying, and I am already starting to feel better. It is so strange that he has this way of making me feel happy when he doesn't even try to.

"There. Now, drink this up and swallow these." He says quietly as he comes back out and sneaks me two pills before handing me the cup of hot coffee with ice in it.

So thoughtful. I don't think I have ever been with a man who gave me anything so sweetly or cared about how I felt.

"Thank you." I reply as I take the pills and then carefully drink a few sips of coffee.

"You are so thoughtful." I add as I begin to look at him in an entirely new light.

A few minutes later, a middle-aged female doctor with long blonde hair, wearing a white doctor's coat comes out and everyone surrounds her to hear the news.

"Tony will be alright. He lost a lot of blood, but the bullet didn't do any real damage. We sewed him up and he should be good to go home tomorrow." She announces authoritatively before asking hesitantly, "Any questions?"

When no one seems to have any, she pulls us aside to ask quietly so only the two of us can hear, "Why was he shot while off duty?  I need to know for my report.  He said nothing when they brought him in, and even now he refuses to really talk about it."

"I can't tell you that.  I found him like he was and there was no one else around.  Perhaps a drive by getting revenge on a cop?" he asks cautiously while trying to put the blame somewhere else.

Obviously, if she knew the truth, we would all be going away for a very long time.

"Well, somehow I doubt that but I have no evidence so I will just put in the paperwork that it was a stray bullet." She murmurs under her breath before walking away.

"We just barely skirted that one." I mention as we walk back to the metal chairs and sit down.

He nods, and then adds quietly, "Tell me about it."

Realizing that I probably should call my grandparents and let them know I am alright, I pull out my phone and scroll to my contacts. When I see grandma on the screen, I press it and then send. Eventually, it starts to ring three times and then I finally hear her worried voice ask, "Justine. Are you O.K.?"

"Yes, grandma. But my father is finally dead." I say with relief but also with sadness in my voice.

"Oh, Justine. I am so sorry. I know you hated him, but he was still your father. Now they are both gone."

There is a silence as I stare down at my hand in my lap and search for the words to say but there is none except, "I am at the hospital with a friend, but I will be home as soon as I can."

"Nancy? Is she alright?" Grandma asks anxiously as her voice starts to rise.

"Oh, no, no. Grandma, I am talking about Tony the cop. You know him. I am here with a bunch of people, and we were just told he is alright. So, it probably won't be too much longer." I say quickly so she doesn't get even more worried.

"Alright then. But make sure you drive home safely. I love you." She says softly before she yawns and ends the call.

With that out of the way, I put the phone away in my pocket and quickly glance over to where Angel is sitting. He seems to be in deep thought about something and now I am wondering exactly what my role is here. Should I stay and hope that he still wants something to do with me? Or do I just leave and never see him again?

Honestly, I don't know if my heart can take a world without Angel in it. So, I sit here silently and wait for him to say something because right now I have no clue where this is going.

"Should you be driving after what happened?" he asks a few minutes later as he looks up from his trance and gazes into my eyes.

"Well, I drove here didn't eye?" I state sarcastically even though I am secretly hoping that he takes me home instead.

"Yes, but now that you have had time to process what has happened, I don't think you should. Maybe you better come back with me tonight to Amy's." he says hesitantly as he seems to weigh his options heavily.

"Amy's?" I think to myself. I certainly hope it isn't his girlfriend or his wife because I don't swing that way and I don't share nicely.

"Amy's?" I ask quietly before he smirks, and I think he realizes where I am going with this.

"Yeah, she basically is my big sister. She married my brother Drift before he died." He says quickly as he looks around the room for someone.

"Oh, that Amy." I say sadly because I didn't want to bring up bad memories, but I am really glad it wasn't one of the two other options.

When I begin to smile, he leans down and cups my chin before he brushes his lips across mine. It was a simple gesture but one that speaks volumes.

"So, after I speak to Trouble quickly, do you want to go back and talk some more?" he asks jokingly after he releases me and leaves me wanting so much more.

I don't think I will ever get over the way he makes me feel when our skin touches.

"Yes, I do." I reply in almost a whisper as I wink at him seductively and then wait for him to take me in more ways than one.

Once he talks with Trouble for a few minutes, we head out. Mind you I have never ridden on a bike in my life, so it is quite entertaining to say the list when I sit on the very back and he says, "Hold on."

At first, I don't wrap my arms around his waist too tightly until he takes off and I almost fall off the back of the bike. When he realizes it, he has to stop quickly and let me scoot back up right next to him before I wrap my arms around his waist tighter this time.

"Are we good now?" he asks as he stares at me intently in the rearview mirror.

"Yes."

He takes off again down the road and the moment I start to relax I feel the vibration between my legs. I smirk before closing my eyes because not only does it feel interesting, but it reminds me of my toy as it rubs against my clit and makes my insides ache for something else entirely. This is shaping up to be one very interesting night.

As he speeds towards the middle of town, I latch around his waist tighter while my pussy begins to throb with every bump. I can tell that he knows before he even says anything because he laughs and then glances in the rearview mirror again when I look up at him.

"Are you alright back there, baby? After all, I would hate to think that my bike gets you off quicker than I do." He says snidely before paying closer attention to the road in front of us.

By the time we pull in the driveway, I have come, and my teeth are clenched tightly on the back of his t-shirt. He turns the key and then takes it out as I am forced to pull myself off him. I have already come to terms with the fact that I am shameless so why not go with it as I say seductively, "I need you to prove you can make me come harder and faster."

He turns around quickly and raises an eyebrow at me as he takes off his helmet and mask. Then he asks sarcastically, "Oh, really. A challenge?"

I nod, and then whisper breathlessly, "Mm, hm."

"Well then I will have to take you up on it." He states quickly as he scoops me up in his arms and then turns to kick the door open.

When we enter the house, a small woman rushes out of a closed room and stares at me as if I am interrupting something.

"Angel. Why is she here?" she asks angrily and then waits for an answer anxiously.

He quickly puts me down on my feet and then lowers his head before he answers softly, "Amy, Brick is dead, and the others are long gone. As for Justine, she is my woman and wherever I go, she does. Tomorrow we will get our own place, but for tonight I need a bed, and it is time to celebrate."

Normally, I would have thought that she would be smiling, but she seems more worried about me being here than her own happiness.

"I am sorry that I am intervening. If you want me to leave, I will go home." I say sadly before Angel takes my hand possessively.

"Enough. There will be no more talk of this. Drift has been avenged and I will be out of your hair tomorrow. As for tonight, you know the rules. If you hear screaming, don't call the cops." He says as he starts to laugh and then scoops me back up and throws me over his shoulder.

## Chapter 20: Getting Legal

"Grandma, I have found a good man, and I am staying at his place tonight. I will be alright." Justine says sweetly as she talks on the phone to her grandma.

She had forgotten to call her back and tell her that she wouldn't be coming home so she did as soon as we entered the room.

"Yes, I know grandma. I love you too." She replies before ending the call and placing it on the nightstand by the bed.

"Good. Now where were we? Oh, yes." I say before picking her up and throwing her further up on the bed.

As she lays there with her raven hair strewn across the pillows, she looks like the most beautiful angel. I can already picture her naked and waiting for me with pierced lips. "Soon, boy, soon." I think to myself as I pull off my clothes and throw them across the room. As soon as I strip out of my briefs my shaft comes to attention instantly while I look at her licking her lips.

She waits for me so patiently so now I must reward her for being a "good girl."

"So, what did you say about faster?" I ask sarcastically as I climb on top of her and straddle her legs before I unbutton her jeans slowly.

"I forget." She says seductively as she plays the game so well.

"Well, I guess you can forget me burying my head between your legs then, can't you?"

When she realizes what I said she quickly changes her tune and shakes her head before she whispers, "Pretty please."

A Cheshire smile spreads across my lips as she reaches for him, but I deny her.

"Nah uh. It is my turn baby. You are so beautiful that I could worship you for days."

I say breathlessly as I begin to wonder what I am thinking.

Quickly I wiggle her pants off and tease her by leaning over and leaving butterfly kisses as I go. When I stop for a second, she opens her mouth and begins to pant. As I lick her inner legs all the way back up, I stop just before I reach her nub and then blow on it softly. Then I rub my nose very gently over it.

She cries out in need as she spreads her legs. "Please. Please, I need you now."

I feel her hands reach for my head and I let her hold on as she shoves me against her soaked pussy tightly as my tongue flicks out and licks her clit hungrily.

"Oh, I need more." She begs as her legs wrap around my neck.

So, I curl my tongue and slip it between her folds.

"Please…." She says breathlessly as her voice drifts off.

I fuck her with it, thrusting in and out quickly. Then when that does not seem to be enough, I bite down on the sensitive skin of her clit before sucking on it harder and harder. She cries out in pain, and she scratches at my head, but then she lets loose and begins to squirt on me. Immediately, I close my eyes when I feel the warm spray cover my face as well as the rest of my mouth before I lick it up and she shivers uncontrollably.

Just to know that I have that effect on her, makes my dick jerk from side to side.

"Alright baby. Now it is time." I say right before I turn her over and then pull her to the edge of the bed.

"Get on all fours for me." I demand forcefully as I grab a handful of her silky hair and wrap it around my fingers.

She does as I ask before I yank her head back violently and then smack her ass with my right hand. It echoes throughout the room as I feel her soft skin underneath my hand.

"Fuck, you feel so good." I say when I grab ahold of my throbbing cock and rub the tip over both entrances.

"Which one now?" I ask her before she thrusts her ass at me and I add, "Mm. I don't think you care. Am I right?"

She quickly shakes her head and glances back at me before I thrust him in her pussy.

"Gawd, it is so sweet I could stay in here forever." I yell as I throw my head back and begin to pound her.

"I am going to make sure you know that you are mine when I fill you with my cum." I state affectionately before I realize the gravity of what I have just said.

I knew all along that I cared for her, but….earlier, I was willing to give up everything to save her life, including my own.

Before I can even think about this on a deeper level, I feel my balls become so hard and then they empty into her as I moan louder than I probably should have. I yell, "Justine" at the top of my lungs and then my legs give out as she tights around me.

"I am coming." She says softly as she shudders against me, and we both fall over onto the bed.

Because I came so hard, I feel completely drained and am unable to move, so I curl up behind her warm body and fall fast asleep. However, when I wake up to someone sucking on my dick early in the morning, I open my eyes and look down at her. As I look closer, I notice that her eyes are closed, and she is sleeping soundly with my cock in her mouth. She is sucking on him gently and snoring in between.

I don't want to wake her, so I try to go back to sleep but find that it is more erotic than anything. So, I lie awake and enjoy the feeling of her mouth on him for what it is until the sun shines brightly on the bed and I come up with a plan.

"Baby, you need to wake up." I say sweetly as I shake her gently and then slip him out of her mouth as she opens her eyes.

"Today is the first day of the rest of our lives. We are going legal, and I know exactly how." I say excitedly as I run my fingers over her cheek bone and then kiss her lips softly before I continue, "I need to head into the club this morning after I make a phone call. But before I do, I will take you back to your grandparents so you can pack your things. Because when I pick you up later, we will have a place of our own. Just you wait and see."

As soon I climb out of bed, I quickly grab my clothes before putting them on. She does the same and the whole time I can't help but to want her. But I know that I need to do this for the sake of my nephew and others, so I call Trouble and have him get them all together.

"Ready?" I ask as she puts on her shoes and then stares at me happily.

"Yes." She replies as she smiles at me with a twinkle in her eyes.

"Shall we?"

She nods, before she walks out the door and I follow behind her.

Once I drop her off at her grandparents, I arrive at the club and go inside. Everyone is there, including Tony. I had made sure to include him because he is an important part of the plan. I need to make sure that there will be no trouble from other gangs or motor clubs until we have a contract with the government in our hands.

While looking around at everyone and smiling, I realize that we will never be the same again as I say loudly so everyone can hear me speak, "The government always needs gun dealers, right? Well, who is better than a biker gang who has connections to the underworld. We already know who and where, we just need a way to get the guns without getting into trouble. This will cut down on territorial disputes because we will have the backing of the U.S. Government. Now, of course, a few sales under the table won't hurt anyone as long as they never find out about it." I pause and then add sarcastically, "Tony, pretend you didn't hear that part."

When I sit down at the head of the table, I take a drink from the half empty bottle of whiskey before asking excitedly, "Now, shall we vote or just go ahead with it?"

For a few minutes everyone begins to talk but then one by one they quiet down and sit still. Austin stands up and then states, "I do believe that the general consensus says go for it."

"Well then good. That is settled. Now, Tony I will need your department to act as protection while this is being enacted because we will be preoccupied with all the b.s. paperwork." I state before I start to laugh.

"No problem. I think we can handle that if you don't start another all-out war like the last." Tony replies breathlessly as he tries to stand.

"Bro. Sit back down. You are in enough pain. This won't happen for at least another few weeks because I must contact the government first and tell them we mean to do business legally. Anyway, get better first. I am going to head out and grab a house for me and my little lady. The rest of you make sure to get drunk for me. After all, it is time to party." I say quickly and then stand up to walk out the door.

No one really bothers, but I can feel all eyes on me before I shut it behind me. I knew that they would not be happy about the two of us, but over time they will get used to it.

"I need to get some fresh air." I murmur under my breath as I get on my bike and start to drive around Crescent Bay.

When I turn the corner of Washington Street, I see it. The perfect house and it has been staring me in the face all along. It's across the street from Amy's and it is so close that it could bite me if it had teeth. But what better way to stay in my nephew's life and to keep an eye on him.

So, after I make sure it is empty, I pick up Justine and use my mask as a blind fold on her before I stop in front of the house and help her down. Instantly, she begins to get excited as she pleads with me, "Please. Can I take it off now?"

I start to laugh and then reply, "Yes. Yes, you can." before I watch her take off the mask and her eyes widen as she looks at me with a confused look in her eyes.

"It is ours. I wanted to stay close enough to my nephew Jonathan to make sure that he is always safe. I hope that is alright?" I ask as I watch her eyes light up and she jumps up and down.

"Yes, of course, yes. It is absolutely perfect."

The End

This Is The End Of Book One In The Road Rangers Series Where Each Road Ranger Gets Their Own Story.

Please see the next in the series as they come out in the next several months by following me on my social media and checking out mdlabelle.com

*I hope you enjoyed Angel. Please review it after reading and then look for my other books.*

# About the Author

M.D. LaBelle is an international award-winning, bestselling multi genre author. Her genres include horror, dark romance, fantasy, thriller, romance, psychological thriller, youth horror, and children's books. They can be found on all major online bookstores, plus some indie bookstores, as well as a few physical ones. She lives in Mount Pleasant, Michigan with her loving husband and 4 out of her 6 children. While she spends most of her time writing, she also has a degree in Art from Central Michigan University and is a violinist. After following her on social media, please check out her books on any of the bookstores and at her website/bookstore at https://www.mdlabelle.com


www.instagram.com/M.D.LaBelle/

Twitter Account

www.twitter.com/MDLaBelle1

Facebook Account

www.facebook.com/profile.php?id=100062142582314

I hope you enjoyed reading Angel. Please take the time to read all my other novels if you haven't already and to keep an eye out for the rest of the series where every book is about a different male character in the group. Thank you.

**Review it.** Please review this novel and let others know what you liked about this book. If you want, please visit me at www.mdlabelle.com

Angel

Book One of The Road Rangers MC Series

Copyright © 2024 M.D. LaBelle

Casper Publishing

All Rights Reserved

This book is a work of fiction. Characters and names are of the author's imagination or are used fictitiously. Any resemblance to an actual person, living or dead, is entirely coincidental.

All rights are reserved. No part of this publication may be reproduced, distributed, or transmitted in any form or by any means, including photocopying, recording, or other electronic or mechanical methods, without the express prior written permission of the publisher, except in the case of brief quotations embodied in critical reviews and certain other noncommercial uses permitted by copyright law. For permission requests, please contact the author through her website: www.mdlabelle.com

www.ingramcontent.com/pod-product-compliance
Lightning Source LLC
LaVergne TN
LVHW061046070526
838201LV00074B/5196